VELVET MIDNIGHT

THE GOLD BROTHERS - BOOK TWO

MAX WALKER

Edited By: ONE LOVE EDITING

BENJAMIN GOLD

This wasn't how I envisioned my life going.

I thought I was going to be a successful sports star, maybe a famous veterinarian, or maybe I'd open up another sanctuary, following in my moms' footsteps.

None of that happened. Life's light seemed to turn off for me, and I was having a really hard time turning the spark back on. I fell into the doldrums and let myself think it was normal.

Then, on my twenty-fourth birthday, in comes the one surprise I wanted most and liked the least: Rex freaking Madison. My older brother's best friend, my first crush, my first time.

And my absolute worst nightmare, walking in on two thick, sexy, tree-trunk like legs and smiling an electrically blue-eyed smile.

Somewhere, deep down under the cobwebs in my chest, a spark lit.

REX MADISON

Well. Crap. This wasn't how I expected things to go.

I'd been coasting, living under my dad's oppressive shadow while using his bank account to keep rent paid and alcohol flowing. I was running, and life caught up to me.

Now, I was being blackmailed for a sex tape I never consented to, and lost my meal ticket to an easy life because of it.

My best friend offered me a place to stay, and I took it. I figured some time at the Gold Animal Sanctuary would help me get things back on track.

One look from Benji was all it took for everything to derail again. It had been six years since we saw each other last, ending an incredible time on a terrible note. Benji had taught me how to love myself--all of myself-- back then, and now I wanted to return the favor, no matter how much time may have separated us from our explosive nights together.

Nights I'd never forget and always ache to repeat.

ALSO BY MAX WALKER

The Gold Brothers

Hummingbird Heartbreak

Velvet Midnight

The Stonewall Investigation Series

A Hard Call

A Lethal Love

A Tangled Truth

A Lover's Game

OR

Books 1-4 Box Set

The Stonewall Investigation- Miami Series

Bad Idea

Lie With Me

His First Surrender

The Sierra View Series

Code Silver

Code Red

Code Blue

Code White

The Guardian Series

Books 1-4 Box Set

Audiobooks:

A Hard Call - narrated by Greg Boudreaux

A Lethal Love - narrated by Greg Boudreaux

A Tangled Truth - narrated by Greg Boudreaux

A Lover's Game - narrated by Greg Boudreaux

Deck the Halls - narrated by Greg Boudreaux

Code Silver - narrated by Jason Frazier

Christmas Stories:

Daddy Kissing Santa Claus

Daddy, It's Cold Outside

Deck the Halls

Receive access to a bundle of my **free stories** by signing up for my newsletter!

Tap here to sign up for my newsletter.

Be sure to connect with me on Instagram and Twitter **@maxwalkerwrites.** And join my Facebook Group: Mad for Max Walker

Max Walker

MaxWalkerAuthor@outlook.com

BENJAMIN GOLD

THE GOLD ANIMAL Sanctuary was decked out for our twenty-fourth birthday. The trees had colorful rainbow streamers hanging from them, and most of the animals were wearing party hats, which looked extra funny on the bouncing Tammy, our North American river otter, who enjoyed hanging out with us more than the dogs did. She was currently playing with my twin brother's shoelace.

"Dusty, I think she's trying to tie your shoes together," I warned.

He laughed and playfully rolled Tammy over on her side. She rolled right back and got to work with laser focus.

Brandon, my brother's husband, laughed a big booming laugh as he walked over to the table. My moms flanked him, laughing equally loud, Mia holding a large golden bag in her hand.

"You guys need to hear Brandon's impression of Donald Duck. It's creepy," Ashley said, sitting down next to me. She put a hand around my shoulders and pulled me into a tight side hug. Her hair smelled like it always did: strawberries and vanilla.

"Happy Birthday, Benj," my mom said, kissing the top of my head. She leaned over and kissed my brother's head next. "Dust, my two loves."

"Happy Birthday, you old fucks," Brandon said in a scarily accurate Donald Duck impression.

The table cracked up as Brandon took his seat next to Dusty. We were outside next to the pool, and I had to admit, looking around at the smiling faces that came together for my birthday made me feel really good. A foreign feeling lately, which made it all the more sweeter.

"All right," Mia said, setting the bag on the table. Uncle Peanut and Aunt Gabbie, two best friends who lived next door and were honorary members of the Gold family, moved their seats over so my mom could take center stage at the table. Uncle Peanut, dressed to the nines, kept checking his watch, which Aunt Gabbie loudly ribbed him about. I didn't mind. He had a date tonight, and the excitement was clear on his face.

Hey, at least someone at this party is gonna get it in.

I rubbed the back of my head and tried not to think too much. That's what ended up getting me in trouble. I wanted to enjoy today, and that meant making a conscious effort to enjoy it. Lately, shit had felt so empty, my life looking like a boring blank canvas, that I almost forgot I even had the ability to enjoy anything.

My sister, Kaitlyn, reached for the golden bag, but my mom pulled it back. The only one missing today was my older brother, Maverick, who said he'd be arriving late.

"Eh, eh, eh," she said, wagging a finger in the air at my sister. "Tradition says birthday boy reaches into the bag first. Since it's a tie, we go by time of birth, and Benji, that means you go."

"Ugh, by five minutes. I'm always behind," Dusty said, rolling his eyes and smiling.

The Gold Grab Bag. My moms' favorite moment at any birthday, and all of ours, too. Inside the bag was a collection of cards, each one with a photo of one of the animals that had been rescued, rehabbed, and released by the sanctuary. On the back of each card was either a challenge or a prize. One of those cards was golden, and whoever pulled that card had their choice of whatever other cards someone else chose. So after three rounds, someone might have accumulated sixty bucks in prize money only to have it snatched away at the very last round from a golden card pick.

It was a fun time and kept a few healthy grudges running in the family.

I reached in and shuffled around a bit, everyone's eyes on me.

"Annnnd," I said, pulling out the card. "It's one of the cheetah cubs." I lifted the card and showed it around the table. On the back, it said, "You now have to pick one person to race two laps around the yard. Winner gets twenty-five dollars."

There were a few choices I could go with. I knew Mia didn't love running, although no one could ever catch her on horseback. Although Uncle Peanut was older, his nickname growing up had been Jack the Crack of Lightning (which he shortened to Jack the Crack sometime in college, a story he loved to tell), so I *definitely* wasn't choosing him. Kaitlyn was also a track star, and Brandon would have smoked me.

But Dusty...

He already saw it coming, standing up with a roll of his eyes. He adjusted his glasses and headed to the start line Ashley pointed to. Even though we were identical twins, the two of us were pretty different. My brother worked for NASA and had a brain the size of an orbiting moon, while I had concentrated on other muscles throughout my life. Lately, though, I'd been slacking with my fitness routine, so it really could have been anyone's game.

Ashley lifted her hand as we lined up. "Ready, set, go!"

And we ran, and we laughed, and I almost tripped. Tammy joined on the second lap, bouncing behind me as Dusty took the lead in a final last-minute push. I saw him pull ahead and dug deep for some more speed.

I took first place at a photo finish. I grabbed Tammy and lifted her up as if we had won the gold in an Olympic race. The table cheered and laughed, and my brother gave me a pat on the back.

Next up was Aunt Gabbie, who pulled out a card of Ari the hawk we rehabbed last year. "You're soaring high and collect a $25 prize." She lifted her hands and wooted, my mom handing over her prize.

"Oh thank the Lord, I thought I would have to get up from my seat for something." She leaned back, making an exaggerated display of counting her winnings.

We spent the next hour or so pulling cards and playing the game, going over the number of rounds we normally played. At one point, I looked around at my family and felt an overwhelming sense of gratitude. It was a reminder of how life used to be, when we were all together, hanging out at the same dinner table every evening, laughing and talking and joking.

It felt so freaking good, I couldn't stop myself from smiling even if I wanted to. This was so different from how I'd been feeling lately, which mainly was just a mixture of numbness and sadness. I couldn't even pinpoint exactly why or when I started feeling that way, but it was eating away at me little by little. It made moments like these seem so few and far between, which meant I just had to savor today as much as I could. I didn't know when the gray waves would hit me, but at least for right now, the sun was shining and the tide had pulled the gray waters away.

We finished up with the Gold Grab Bag and settled into a relaxed mood. The sun was still high in the sky, but the fresh fall breeze kept us from getting too hot.

"Benji, want to go throw around the football?" Brandon asked, leaning over Dusty. Dusty gave his husband a kiss on the neck. Those two couldn't have been more perfect for each other, brought together by a fire and still burning hot all these years later.

"Yeah, let's do it." If I even still remembered how to throw a ball. I used to love playing sports and was actually damn good at most of the ones I committed to. Football and wrestling had been big ones in high school. In college I'd started playing soccer and tennis, loving both of them but dropping them sometime after graduation.

Brandon, a world-famous rugby player and popular

internet personality, probably wouldn't have trouble throwing the ball.

We got up from the table, Brandon taking one last bite of cake and leaving the empty plate on the table. Before we could even leave the table, my mom called out, "It's Mav!"

Coming from out of the house was my older brother, a carry-on suitcase in his hand and a bottle of water in the other.

Maverick waved, calling out to the table. He looked like he had just rolled out of bed, wearing a pair of gray sweats and a black T-shirt with impenetrable shades on his face, his honey-brown hair messed up in the way it always was when my brother was fighting a hangover. I'd seen that look a lot, which only made me appreciate him being here even more.

I got up from my seat and went over to him, Dusty close behind me. He opened his arms and wrapped me into a hug.

"Happy Birthday, little bro."

"Thanks for coming," I said. Maverick lived in New York, which wasn't too far a flight from our house here in Georgia, but still, it was a flight, and when your head was sloshed with vodka and beer and whatever else Maverick chugged last night, then an hour-and-a-half flight could easily feel like a ten-hour flight.

"Of course, Benj." His smile slanted into an expression I recognized. My brother always looked like that when he was about to drop some kind of bomb. He loved doing that.

"Check it out—I brought you a birthday surprise all the way from New York."

Mav stepped aside, his arms looking like a game-show prize presenter, aiming toward the sliding glass doors leading into the house.

I looked, half expecting my brother to have hired the cast of *Magic Mike* to strut out through the doors. I braced myself to die from embarrassment, knowing that my moms would be watching as their twins sat down for birthday lap dances from impossibly cut (and impossibly flexible) men.

And then the surprise turned the corner, walking out with a much bigger suitcase rolling behind him. I had to do a double take, squinting my eyes, unsure if who I saw was really who I thought.

"Happy Birthday, Benji," he said.

Rex Madison waved at me with a smile on his face.

Rex Madison, my brother's best friend.

Rex Madison, my first ever crush.

Rex Madison, the one I lost my virginity to.

Rex Madison, the one who irreparably broke my heart and disappeared for six whole fucking years.

I turned and walked away, hurried, trying to get as far from Rex Madison as I possibly could.

2

REX MADISON

FORTY-EIGHT HOURS EARLIER

THE ENTIRE CITY of New York twinkled and glittered underneath me.

Pretty much the same way Penelope's eyes twinkled underneath me, her big doe-like brown eyes going wide as I pushed in deeper down her throat.

"That's it, baby." I grabbed a fistful of her hair and directed her head, making sure her lips were getting every inch of me. Her makeup smeared just enough to make my balls even tighter. Too much and I would have felt like I was hooking up with the Joker. Thankfully, her mascara seemed waterproof.

"Swallow it." I looked through the floor-to-ceiling window, feeling like the king of the motherfucking world.

I opened my legs a little wider. Her fingernails

pressed into my thighs as she tried to deep-throat me again, gagging right before her tongue reached my nuts.

The warmth of her mouth, the way her tongue slid up and down my shaft, the way she sounded like a drowning vacuum—it was almost enough to make me blow.

Almost.

One thing was missing, though.

A knock came from the locked door. My date for the hour looked over, my cock still splitting her jaw.

"That must be our second guest." I let go of the reins, dropping her silky blonde hair back down over her bare shoulders. She stood, wiping her lips with a smile. I kissed her, loving the salty taste of me on her tongue.

I crossed the large bedroom, my toes sinking into the plush gray rug, my hard cock swinging left and right. From the other side of the door, I could hear the loud sounds of a party still going strong, even though the clock on the bedside table said it was close to four in the morning.

I put a hand on the brass doorknob and rapped a knuckle three times against the door. I counted four seconds before three more knocks answered me from the other side.

It was him.

I unlocked the door and opened it, making sure to step behind it so that no one could see my bare naked ass and my rock-hard dick.

"Hey, Scott," Penelope said in a hungry tone. She had moved onto the bed, crawling on her fours with her ass up in the air, her hair falling down onto the white sheets like a golden waterfall. She was a beautiful girl, and a goddess at giving blowjobs. The way I leaked a string of precome and saliva onto the floor was proof of that.

But the second Scott walked into the room, my attention (and desire) shifted.

The guy was a beast, his shirt straining with the bulging biceps and powerful chest, a sprinkling of dark hair showing through the undone buttons of his shirt. His jawline was a mixture of straight lines and hard curves that made my mouth water and my cock jerk. He wore a tight pair of light jeans that hugged his bulge so tight, I thought his cock was about to tear right through it.

I closed the door and locked it, standing naked underneath the dim light, licking my lips as Scott immediately began to undress, his hazel-green eyes drinking me in like he'd just found the last Coke bottle in the desert. Penelope leaned over on the bed and helped him with his shirt.

I got down and focused on the meat of the situation, rubbing my face into Scott's growing bulge, his jeans now a puddle on the floor, his white briefs doing a terrible job of holding back his erection.

Thankfully.

I licked the head of his cock, poking out from his underwear. I sucked him into my mouth and stroked him over the soft fabric, closing my eyes and drinking him in, relishing the feel of his cock between my lips. I fucking loved it. If I could live off sucking dick for the rest of my life, I would in a cock-hungry heartbeat.

Instead, I had to live my life hiding this part of me, keeping locked up inside of a room, waiting for a secret knock so I could get my fix.

Scott fell back onto the bed. I didn't waste a second, pulling off his briefs and getting him fully naked, my mouth drooling at the sight of him springing free. Penelope sat behind him, rubbing his chest and kissing his neck.

"Sorry for dragging you out of the party," I said, my smirk showing that I had zero regrets.

"Penelope's text came at the perfect time. I'd been wanting this for weeks."

"I know, so have I." I leaned in and kissed his inner thigh, loving how the hair on his legs felt against my lips.

"What happened?" His question sounded simple enough, but the answer was real fuckin' complicated.

"Don't worry about it."

"I won't," he said, gasping as I took him in my mouth, swallowing him down to the base. If deep-throating were an Olympic sport, I would have for sure won the gold about sixty-nine times over. Sponsorships would have been through the roof. "Just do it" would have taken on a whole other meaning.

Scott grabbed the back of my head. It drove me even more wild, swallowing and gobbling like it was a free buffet. The bed shifted as Penelope moved to the chair, her hands gliding up and down her own body, her eyes half-lidded with passion.

Ever since we had started this arrangement, she always liked sitting back and watching. I asked a few different times if I could help get her off, but she said her fingers and our sweaty cocks rubbing together was all she needed.

Yeah. My life wasn't exactly black and white, and that was exactly how I wanted it.

"Oh, Rex, that's it. Wow, holy shit." Scott's eyes rolled back. I moved onto the bed, the memory foam mattress barely shifting under our combined weight.

"Jesus, you're so fucking sexy," Scott said, looking up at me with wide green eyes. He licked his lips and leaned up, his hands rubbing my body, squeezing and kneading and massaging. "I love how much of a bear you are." The way Scott's cock leaked proved he wasn't lying.

I let him rub me up and down, worshiping the curves and hair and chest.

I fucking loved it. Years ago, this would have made me self-conscious about a hundred times over. There'd been a long period in my life when my weight had become my biggest issue. Something I obsessed over and was constantly bullied over, constantly reminded about. The snide comments only enforced the view I'd see whenever I looked in the mirror.

Not anymore. These days, I embraced my bearness.

Some might say overweight, others would say fluffy, but of the people I really cared about, most would say fucking perfect. It took me a second to figure out what being a bear meant, considering I was so deep in the closet I might as well have turned into a coat hanger.

Being a bear means being a bigger man with a chest of curly hair and ample amount of options to grab during sex.

Being a bear *does not* mean having the barest layer of fat, which was something I recently heard that made me roll my eyes back into the dawn of time.

Tonight, Scott was in the "fucking perfect" camp, rubbing my body with a hunger in his gaze. He rubbed and sucked and kissed and licked. His breath felt warm against my stomach as he nibbled on me, gyrating his hips onto the bed, pushing my legs further apart. I throbbed against his chest, his heartbeat matching the pulse of my cock.

"Fuck," I hissed, letting my head fall back onto the pillow. Penelope was sitting on the leather chair against the window, her legs open and her eyes drinking us up, the way she bit her lip, revealing just how much pleasure coursed through her.

The lights of the city were bright enough to shine into the dark room, one hundred and one stories above the ground. This was one of the tallest buildings in the city, and I currently lived in the penthouse next door. Francisco was a wild neighbor to have, that was for sure. An heir to some oil fortune and an addict to lavish parties dripping wall to wall with supermodels of all genders, it really helped justify the crazy amount of rent I paid.

A red light stuck out from the sea of blinking, artificial stars. It seemed to be floating. Like a UFO or something. It blinked on and off. It reminded me of something...

Wait a fucking second.

I looked to the opposite side of the room, at a bookshelf that took up an entire wall. Filled with random bullshit, it would have been real easy to miss the blinking red light.

I was looking for it, though.

And I found it.

"What the fuck is that?" I pushed Scott off me, his lips leaving a wet circle on my neck.

Scott and Penelope both followed my gaze. "What's what?" Penelope asked.

"That blinking red light. Between the globe and the lockbox."

I stood, my face flushing with blood. Closer inspection wasn't needed, but still, I had to see it for myself.

Had to know how truly fucked things were.

Behind the antique globe and scratched-up bronze lockbox was a tiny camera, the blinking light coming from above the lens. Everything had been recorded. Everything.

I snatched the camera off the shelf, the globe dropping to the floor and breaking in half. The camera flew through the air, cracking against the window. It fell to the floor in pieces. Penelope and Scott both looked shocked, their faces turning paper pale, their jaws dropping in unison.

"Did either of you do this?" I felt a fury welling inside me like the tide being yanked by a full moon.

Scott shook his head while Penelope uttered a "hell no."

"Tell me the fucking truth."

Scott spoke up. "We didn't. I didn't— Why would we?" Penelope was picking up the pieces of the camera, shock playing out on her face.

I rubbed a hand over my face, hoping that the entire world would have disappeared by the time I opened my eyes.

It didn't.

"I need to go." Everything moved in slow motion and on fast forward at the same time. It felt like my limbs didn't belong to me. Like I was watching someone else tug on their jeans and shirt, except I was watching it through their eyes. This moment didn't feel real. Like I was drowning in oil and burning from the inside all at once.

I threw the door open. The sounds of the party echoed the beating of my pulse inside my skull. Dodging offers of drinks and conversation, I made it down the packed hall and into the main living room.

I was looking for Francisco, scanning the writhing room of bodies and disco lights. Instead, I found Maverick Gold, my best friend and probably the one person I needed most in that moment.

He must have seen the expression on my face. He

crossed through the room, his charismatic smile quickly flipping into a worried frown the closer he got to me.

"What's wrong?" he asked, speaking over the thumping music.

"Everything." I had to sit down. My knees felt like giving out. "Everything's wrong. Everything's over."

3

BENJAMIN GOLD

"OH WHAT THE HELL, BRO." I turned and walked off.

"Why are you briskly running away?" Dusty asked, catching up to me.

I realized he had to *catch up to me*, so I slowed it down. "I'm not running away. I just remembered I have something else to do, and it's uh, somewhere else."

We didn't need our twin-ception powers for Dusty to see that I was full of complete shit.

"He seemed surprised to see you?"

"He did?" I caught my heart skipping a beat, making me want to bang my head against a nearby tree stump. "Well, that's stupid, considering this is my family's sanctuary he decided to show up at like some kind of stray."

"Whoa," Dusty said, looking over at me. He wore

his thick-framed Ray-Ban glasses, his eyes magnified underneath the lenses. "I didn't realize he'd bring up so much emotion."

"Yeah. Me either."

We had walked all the way to the stables, which were dusted over with a gentle blanket of snow. There were hoof prints in the pasture, leading toward the covered trough of hay. There, four of my mom's new rescue horses munched away on their lunch. They were a mixture of grays and whites and browns, all four of them found abandoned in the same manure-filled pen.

I had already spent the morning grooming all four of them and instead led my brother down the path to the right, where another stable linked up to a separate pen. This was where Electra lived, a grumpy old thing that fought anyone who wasn't a Gold, horses included. My mom had put a pink-and-blue-dotted birthday hat on her, which looked comically small on her massive head.

I smiled, a genuine smile that almost caught me off guard. "Hey there, lady." I reached into a nearby bag and pulled out an apple.

Dusty leaned on a post as Electra whinnied her big gray head over the rail of her stable. She shook her head and bared her teeth in a hungry smile.

"What's he even doing here?"

My brother shrugged. "Judging from the packed bags, it looks like he's been offered to stay here. That's just a hypothesis, obviously. You ran off so fast, I wasn't even able to say hi to the guy."

"And on my birthday. What a jerk. He clearly hasn't changed."

"Right," Dusty said, looking down at his sneakers.

Electra grabbed the apple from my palm, the loud crunches that followed working as well as those addictive whispering videos I sometimes watched. Or the videos with the people cutting through clean layers of colored sand. Those got me hooked for hours.

"Are you ever going to tell me what happened between you two?"

I put my head against Electra's, rubbing her cheek. No one else would have been able to do this without getting a stars-out kind of head-butt from her.

"You already know what happened," I said.

Most of it.

"Yeah, but Benji, come on. I know you. Something else happened in Costa Rica. I know you two kissed but... why this reaction? Why the anger?"

"Because he's as closed-minded as the family he comes from, and he said some stupid shit. Shit I can't forget." I went to grab another apple from the bag. Electra clopped in a little happy dance that made me want to do one in return.

Animals always had that kind of effect on me. I could be in the middle of a roaring storm and still feel comforted by a nuzzle from Electra or a cuddle with Tammy.

"Maybe he's changed, Benj. People change."

"I doubt it. Not with the way his dad's been acting, trending every other day for some new dumb 'save the family' speech."

"That's his father, not him. Plus, he's up for reelection, isn't he? All that bullshit is going to float to the surface during times like these." Dusty came over to my side and pet Electra's head, rubbing the spot between her eyes. "Has anything been said about him?"

"I don't know, I don't keep tabs on them. His dad's just such a big name, it's hard to ignore."

"Maybe he does ignore it, then. Maybe he's not even involved with it."

"Maybe—"

Another voice cut in. One as familiar as my own and still stranger than a random passerby. "Maybe I got into a fight with my father and it's the reason why I've pretty much lost everything, having to take my best friend's—your brother's—offer of staying at his family's sanctuary for a few weeks." Rex lifted a hand and—fuckin' hell—he smiled. Not just any smile either. It was the kind of smile that implanted itself deep into your brain, like a brand that marked a lifetime commitment to a sunshine and sex cult.

If I wasn't so embarrassed at being overheard by him, I would have probably started to actively drool.

"Rex, I, uh, we uhm, we were just talking about you." I motioned between my twin and me, completely lost for words. I wasn't expecting this. None of it. All I had been looking forward to was a generous portion of vanilla-and-strawberry birthday cake and a long, substantial nap, followed by a *Matrix* movie rewatch that I had planned to last until at least four in the morning, around the time I'd be able to go to sleep.

Yeah, that's what I had planned for my twenty-fourth birthday. Not... not all this.

"It's good to see you, Rex." Dusty offered a hand to shake. My twin was dwarfed by Rex's six-foot-three stature, his presence made even larger by those ocean-blue eyes and pillow-sized lips. He had short dark hair that caught the sunshine in bright highlights.

Dusty and I weren't mirror images of each other. There had come a point in college where I dove into sports and fitness while my brother focused more on his smarts and succeeding at pretty much anything he ever put his mind to, something I was finding difficult lately. So while Dusty may have looked tiny and pocket-sized next to Rex, I felt more... well, more like a perfect fit.

"I'm gonna go check on the cleanup." Dusty dipped, waving over his shoulder as he walked away, back toward the yard.

The stable felt a hundred times smaller. I wanted to rear up like a pissed-off Electra and run into unbound pastures, running far away from Rex Madison and his perfect freakin' face, framed by that perfect head of hair, with that perfect fuckin' beard.

Instead, I said, "You look good."

Not exactly running, but whatever.

He bit his lip. The fucking asshole bit his lip. "Is that what you were saying about me?"

"No, I actually wasn't." *Okay, find your footing.* Rex was good at disarming me, always had been. Ever since we were teens, when he'd come into my life as my brother's best friend, when he was completely forbidden from me.

And when he also seemed to be completely straight.

Funny how quickly all that changed.

Just one night. One sweaty, steamy, unforgettable tropical night was all it took for me to find out the truth.

"I was just wondering why you were here, that's all. From everything I see online, your life in New York is pretty great."

Rex huffed. "We all know how accurate online photos are." He moved to Electra, slowly. The large thoroughbred horse hadn't stomped off, surprisingly. She stood there, the sun shining on her dappled gray body, her silky mane falling like a waterfall. She was looking at Rex with liquid amber eyes, studying him from head to toe. "Right, Electra?" Rex put a gentle hand on her snout.

I braced myself for a snort and a head whip, but nothing happened.

"She remembers you."

"It hasn't been that long, Benji. You're acting like I crawled out of an ancient crypt."

"Six years is a long time."

"Six years and a day might be the perfect amount of time."

I arched a brow but was able to suppress an eye roll. Aside from always having devastating good looks, Rex also had a tendency to sound like a walking fortune cookie. Sometimes, his nuggets of wisdom were golden, and other times they were the leftover nuggets that fell out of the bag and rolled under the refrigerator.

This was one of the refrigerator nuggets. Still, I'd bite.

"Has it really been six years and a day since you've been here?"

"I moved to New York the day before your birthday. Six years ago."

"Damn, and I was just throwing that 'six' out at random." I huffed a laugh. That wasn't entirely true. I knew damn well it had been six years but I wasn't about to pull out my calendar for him. "Well, you've clearly always had perfect timing."

"I don't know about that," he said. "If I did, I think I would have shown up sooner."

My brow arched and my face cracked, revealing my thoughts without needing very many words at all.

Then why didn't you, Rex? Damn it. Why didn't you?

4

REX MADISON

BENJI LOOKED EXACTLY how I remembered him and, at the same time, completely different from the boy who had taught me so much about myself years ago. He still had the same bright eyes that never failed to lighten up a room, and he still carried himself with his shoulders high and chin proud, even when I could tell all he wanted to do was bury his hand in the sand.

There was a shadow of something else in his eyes. He turned his gaze down at the hay-covered floor, breaking eye contact and leaving me wondering if this was a good idea after all.

"You've been good?" I asked, trying to break the glacier between us. Electra gave a gentle whinny before clopping away to the trough of food.

"I've been all right." Benji leaned against a wooden

post, the brushes clinking together. A midafternoon ray of sunlight cut through an opening in the stable's roof, cutting across his face like the brush of some masterful Renaissance painter.

"All right? I haven't seen you in six and some years and you're going to give me the equivalent of signing 'HAGS, KIT' in my yearbook."

"HAGS?"

"Have a great summer. Yeah, I know, I thought it was a slur at first, too."

Benji laughed at that. Short but sweet, making me want more almost immediately. "KIT is what I should have done with you."

"That means 'Keep Insider Trading,' right?"

My turn to laugh. "Yes, that and 'keep in touch.' It's interchangeable."

He kicked at some imaginary rock on the ground, his gaze flitting from me to the field behind me. "A lot's happened since we last talked. Since Costa Rica."

There it was. The trip. A life-changing trip that altered the course of my happiness and opened my eyes to what I truly wanted. I had temporarily escaped my dad's oppressive shadow, and with Benji's help, I found myself.

It only took me a few days back home for me to lose myself all over again, losing Benji in the process.

And it seemed like time hadn't healed this wound, not with the way he looked at me. He was angry. Same way I felt with how things shook out.

"How about you?" Benji asked.

How about me. "Where do I even start..."

"Let's start with why you're here." Benji crossed his arms. His biceps bulged with the movement. Since when did little Benji turn into built Benji? I remember the day we first met, back when we were teens, and I thought I'd have an impossible time telling the difference between him and Dusty. They were the same exact lanky build with the same dimpled cheeks and bright eyes.

Not anymore. Sometime between our trip to Costa Rica and now, Benji must have found a passionate love for protein shakes and bench-presses, changing him from a twink to a twunk—the muscular version of his formerly skinny but still small-framed self.

I shrugged. "It's a messy story."

"My favorite kind." Benji narrowed his gaze and kept eye contact.

I didn't want to talk about it. The shit hit the fan only two days ago. Everything still felt fresh, like my cuts were all still bleeding. I went from feeling like I had the world in the palm of my hand to having my entire world thrown into a trash disposal. One second,

I was living in the most expensive building in all of New York, and the next, I was staring at a negative bank account and wondering where the fuck I was going to sleep that night.

"My dad and I got into an argument." And the gold medal for oversimplification goes to... me. "I needed a place to lay low for a little, and your brother offered the guesthouse."

Benji arched a brow. Ever since we were kids, he had an innate ability to cut right through whatever bullshit I was serving up on a steaming plate. Was he going to dig further? Would I have opened up more?

Didn't matter. He shrugged and turned, leaving me there with my jaw half-open. "All right," he said, not even turning around. "Hope things get sorted for you."

"Hey, wait up."

Although the view of Benji from the back side was something I wouldn't mind memorizing, I wanted to talk to his front.

He stopped at the entrance to the stable. The wind whipped with a renewed vigor here, stinging at my ears and nose. I stuffed my hands in my pockets and looked down into Benji's eyes, wondering what thoughts swirled behind them. He'd always been a difficult one to read. As a politician's son, I'd met a shit-ton of different people and learned how to get a good read on most everyone within a few minutes of speaking to them. Were they there with ulterior political motives? Were they trying to dig for information, or were they genuinely interested in conversation?

I couldn't get anything on Benji besides *he's pissed.* And he was pissed at me.

"Benji, listen, it's been years since Costa Rica—"

"And?"

"And, I wanted to say—"

"Sorry?"

Damn, he'd gotten way feistier over the years.

"Actually, I wanted to say that I've changed."

He rolled his eyes walked away. Fuck. I sped up and matched his pace as he strolled down the brick path that led toward the main house. Ashley's mouth-watering lasagna must have been on the menu tonight judging by the intoxicating scent growing stronger.

"I've changed, Benji," I said, continuing my train of thought. "I'm not the same kid anymore, and neither are you."

"I'm not so sure about that."

"Huh?"

"You still can't apologize for shit." Benji stopped in his tracks, turning to me. His expression twisted in disappointment, and I immediately regretted everything I had said.

Still, I was a stubborn motherfucker, and "sorry" had always been a very limited word in my vocabulary. Especially since what had happened between us wasn't exactly a cut-and-dry situation. I held a thorn in my side from how shit went down, and part of me wanted to hear *Benji* be the one to say sorry.

Maybe that was my dad's fault, too. Learning that an apology always equaled an admission, even when there had been nothing to admit.

"I'm sorry," I said, "that you still feel hurt from what went down in Costa Rica. I feel the same way."

"Jesus Christ." Another roll of his eyes. He walked away again.

Fuck. I wasn't exactly expecting a beautiful and heartfelt reunion between the two of us, but I certainly wasn't expecting this type of animosity and resentment. A split second had me thinking I should walk the opposite direction, toward the guesthouse and away from the steaming Benjamin Gold. It would likely be the easier option, the one with less friction. I could take a shower and rest up before I put my head down and focused everything on what my next move would be. On how I could stop that damn fucking tape from leaking, and how I could get a sliver of my old life back.

...

I followed behind Benji instead.

"Wait up."

He walked faster.

"Benji, hold on."

He stopped, but not because of me. Tammy the adopted river otter came over running, almost barreling over herself as she came to a dust-filled stop by Benji's feet. He crouched down and gave her some back scratches before she hopped over to me, giving a squeal of excitement. My reaction to her familiar sounds came at me like an unexpected car wreck. I almost started to cry. Actually fucking cry. This otter and the twunk behind her were about to make me weep like a little baby.

I chewed the inside of my cheek as I bent down, using the opportunity to reunite with Tammy as a way to cover the wetness building in my eyes.

"She remembers you," Benji said, sounding a little less tense than the moments before.

"She does." I managed to keep my voice steady. Had to try for more than just two words, though. "She's just like how I remember her, too."

There, and my voice only cracked once. Barely even notic—

"Are you about to cry?"

"What? No. I'm fine. It's fine." I kept my face down, as if I were looking at Tammy and not hiding the tear that slipped down my cheek.

How'd things end up like this?

"It's fine if you do. Animals have the same effect on me, too." Benji crouched down to my level, although I didn't meet his eyes. He started to pet Tammy, who had rolled onto her back, showing us her lighter-colored belly for some scratches. Her fur, resistant to water and cold temperatures, was as dense as a thick winter coat and as soft as silk, an odd and comforting combination.

As comforting as Benji's cologne, drifting my way. And the feel of his fingertips brushing against mine.

Another tear streaked down my cheek. My throat started to tighten, my chest following suit.

Fuck. Fuck!

It all started hitting me at once: the tape. My father. Benji and our trip to Costa Rica. Everything that happened there. The fight. The laughter. The yearning.

The sleepless night; the velvet midnight.

It was my turn to stand and abruptly leave. I couldn't take this. I had to be alone. Needed space to process it all. I walked down the path leading toward the guesthouse, keeping my head down, shaking it slightly, trying to get breaths into my lungs again. Behind me, Benji called out to me.

"Rex. Rex, stop."

"I need a minute." It was all I could squeeze

through my throat. Barely audible, but the crunching of Benji's shoes on the fallen autumn leaves stopped.

I spent the rest of that day and the next locked inside the guesthouse, curtains drawn, as if the thin white sheets would somehow protect me from the waves of panic and sadness that periodically crashed over me, stealing my breath and crushing my heart.

5

BENJAMIN GOLD

SIX YEARS AGO

THE SOUND of the ocean waves relaxed me.

We were sitting on the Costa Rican beach, tiki torches lighting up the area. Mav set up a table on the sand so we could all play dominos and hang out. We'd spent all day helping build a new monkey habitat, and tomorrow we were supposed to work all day on cleaning up another one, so relaxing by the beach with my family and some dominoes was *pretty* perfect.

Oh, and yeah, there was also Rex.

There was always Rex.

Was I obsessed with him? Possibly. Was I ever going to get with him? Absolutely freaking not. He was my brother's best friend and was obviously straight with all the girlfriends he's had. I realized pretty early on that I was gay, and I figured I'd be able to pick up on any kind of clues if Rex had an interest in guys. I was pretty observant that way. Not as observant as my brother, Dusty, since he was like a freaking Nobel Prize–winning scientist and would be able to know everything about anything in only a few minutes... but still, I thought I at least had a decent gaydar.

Rex was nowhere on it. Not even a little pity ping.

So fine, I decided to drool over him from afar, while accepting the fact that I'd never be able to put my hands on his chest and my lips on his lips and my—

"Benji, it's your turn."

"Oh, right, right." I grabbed my double nine and unloaded that sucker, leaving me with a two and a zero. Looking around the table, it looked like I also had the least amount of dominos. I was winning, even with the dickstraction sitting across from me.

God, those eyes.

How were they so blue? And that smile, too.

Ugh.

"What's on the agenda for tomorrow?" Rex asked.

"I think we're going to help with putting up the Christmas decorations, so Benj, that means you're going to go all rogue dictator on us until everything looks perfectly Christmassy," my sister, Kaitlyn, said, knowing me so, *soo* well.

I shot her a sarcastic smile. "It's not my fault you guys don't know how to properly decorate for one of the best—no, *the* best—holiday there is."

"I still think I like Thanksgiving more," my mom, Mia, said, putting a hand around Ashley and kissing the side of her hand. "But I'm biased."

Thanksgiving had been when they first met, so sure, I'd let them have their thing.

Still thought Christmas was better, though.

A warm kind of happiness floated through me as I looked around the table at the people I loved the most in this world. Dusty and I hadn't had the easiest childhood, but being a Gold more than made up for all the bullshit.

This had been a Gold family trip, so we were all here, even Momma Ash, who had been working a really big case these last few weeks. And yes, "family" also included Rex. He'd been my brother's friend since I could remember, and he'd been around us all long enough to be considered as one of us. Being a family of adopted kids taught us early that the real bonds were the ones made in the heart and not the blood. Plus, his own family didn't sound nearly as welcoming or accepting as ours, so he hung out with us more often than not. That meant coming on our yearly volunteer trips. Last year it had been to Belize and the year before that was to Kenya, which was where I first remember drooling over Rex after he had taken off his shirt to work on cleaning an animal enclosure. Dusty called me out about sixty-nine times for breaking my neck in Rex's direction, which, coincidentally, was exactly the kind of move I had been picturing between me and—

"Benj, yoo-hoo? Are you with us, or are you having some prophetic vision about the end of the world?" Mav asked, waving his hand in front of my face.

Rex laughed, the sound hitting me deep in the gut. I looked his way, smiled, blushed, and plopped down one of my last pieces.

"Nah, just a vision of me winning the game."

"Ohh," Rex said, placing one of his pieces down. "He's cocky tonight."

"Always."

It was Dusty's turn. He dropped his last piece and raised his hands in victory. "About that vision," he said, smiling as everyone else revealed the last pieces they had.

"You guys are twins, I can see how he got it confused," Rex said, laughing, making me blush again.

Damn it. That has to stop.

I cracked my neck and looked around. We sat on the peaceful beach, the sound of the waves crashing onto shore not far from us. In the other direction was the small community we were staying at, centered around La Nube Wildlife Sanctuary, or the Cloud Wildlife Sanctuary. From somewhere off in the distance, Pipo, the rescued jaguar, gave a sleepy-sounding roar.

"All right, guys." I stood, deciding to follow Pipo's lead. "I'm headed to bed."

My declaration was met with multiple "sames" and "yeah, me toos." We cleared up the table and put the game away, my brother gloating about his third win in a row. I rolled my eyes listening to him, which Rex had seemed to catch.

"You can't win them all," he said, bumping me with a shoulder.

"When my brother's involved, you can't win *at all*."

"That's not true. I saw you smoke everyone's time in the relay race we had earlier. And you kill it on the basketball court. Plus football."

"And soccer."

Rex smiled. *Damn it.* "And soccer." We started walking toward the building we were staying in. The builders had been so concerned about the forest around the area that they even constructed the house *around* two trees, instead of taking them down, which meant that there was one massive tree trunk in the living room and another through the kitchen.

I freaking loved it.

The rooftop garden was probably my favorite part. It attracted all kinds of crazy cool wildlife. I'd sat there for fifteen minutes tops earlier in the day and counted about four different species of monkey and ten different kinds of reptiles, from colorful geckos to harmless snakes. And the birds, holy crap the birds, they were everywhere, and their songs added a permanent relaxation soundtrack that promised me some bomb-ass naps later.

"We should play tomorrow," Rex said. We stopped on the stairs leading up into the house. For it being December, the air felt warm and thick with humidity.

"I'm down," I said.

"You're gonna have to go easy, though. Running isn't my favorite thing to do." Rex rubbed the back of his head and chuckled, a move that lifted his shirt and showed a peek of skin. Thankfully, it was pretty dark out here, so this time my blush stayed hidden.

"I'll keep it easy."

"Okay, good." Rex leaned on the white wooden railing. "You know, Benji, I'm really proud of you. I remember meeting you and you were like a little twig. I thought the wind would blow too hard and we'd have to tape you back together. But you've really worked hard, and it shows. Watching you run like lightning down a field is crazy and really fucking inspiring."

The moonlight broke through some of the dense canopy, shining like a spotlight on those ocean blues of his.

...

Damn. He left me speechless.

Get it together. Brother's best friend. Straight. Unavailable.

That jolted some words back into my head. "You're really fucking inspiring." Those weren't the words that had landed in my head.

"Really? Nah, I don't think so."

There was a sense of sudden defeat in his tone, which caught me off guard. Rex always dripped in confidence. He was the kind of guy who rarely ever admitted defeat until there wasn't a choice. I'd watched him work his ass off at our house, studying for months at the dining room table. Even on days I could tell were heavy on him, he always powered through. And he scored in the top 5 percent of *all* LSAT takers, which opened up a shit-ton of doors for him.

"You're in a top law school, working your way up to be a big-shot attorney, *and* you make some kick-ass waffles. You've got plenty that inspires me."

Way more than I just listed actually.

Rex put a hand on his stomach, his gaze dropping. "Law school isn't exactly going great, and, well, the waffles may be part of the bigger problem, if you know what I mean."

I knew what he meant, and I hated to see it affecting him so much. Rex was bigger than the average guy, but that didn't mean anything besides the fact that his genes had him holding on to some extra weight than others. I was a witness to it. I probably inhaled double the amount of food Rex would eat, and yet my physique had stayed similar, only fluctuating from skinny to muscular. And it wasn't like Rex would be considered unhealthy or dangerously overweight by any means.

"Rex, you shouldn't have to worry about that. You're perfect the way you are." *Okay, pump the brakes before I tell him I love him and am carrying two of his children.* "You look good, and I don't think there's a problem with your weight at all."

"Thanks, Benj." His smile almost knocked me off my feet. "That means a lot. Sometimes, all I hear is the negative stuff, even if it's just me saying them and not my lovely stepmother saying them."

"Don't listen to her. Or anyone else who has shit to say. It's just them pushing their own crap on you, and you don't have to take it."

"Damn, look at you, a sports star and a star therapist."

"You got a two-for-one deal, tonight."

"Not bad."

Was he moving closer to—yup, he was moving closer to me. Like really close. Like I could feel his breath on me close.

"Can I?" he asked. And I knew what he wanted. I wanted it, too.

I nodded, and that was all it took. He leaned in, and he kissed me, and it felt like my first ever kiss all over again. A rush of emotions almost carried me away into the tide. His lips felt so good against mine, his hand falling onto mine on the rail. Somewhere in the distance, a monkey howled as if cheering us on.

We broke apart when we heard the crunch of rocks from around the bend in the trail, along with the voices of the rest of the family. They turned the corner in the next moment, Dusty spotting me first, waving.

Again, it being dark helped hide how red my cheeks felt and how wet I was sure my lips looked. No one asked why the two of us were hanging out awkwardly on the steps up to the house, and no one asked why I stayed mostly silent for the rest of the night. Rex had gone straight to bed, which left me mostly wondering if that was the only thing "straight" about Rex after all.

6

REX MADISON

THE CLATTER of dishes and the smell of soap was nice. It helped keep me from obsessively checking my phone every other five minutes, wondering if and when and how the video would leak. Would it be through a free porn website, or would someone have set up some paywall so they could profit off my stolen moment of intimacy— No. Focus on the tower of dishes that needed washing, not on the guillotine hanging over my head by a single little thread.

"You really don't have to do this," Mia said at my side, her auburn hair tied up in a messy bun.

"Trust me, I do." I handed down another washed plate. Mia passed it to Benji, who had a drying station set up down the counter. "You've all been so kind in letting me stay here. It's the least I can do."

I'd been at the Gold Sanctuary for about two weeks

now, and I felt eternally grateful to Mia and Ashley for letting me stay. I had made some fucked-up turns in life, but Mia, Ashley, and the rest of the Golds had always been there to right those turns since I was a sixteen-year-old kid.

Now, at twenty-six, as a law school dropout with a nearly zero balance bank account and a rising mountain of credit card debt made worse by the abandonment of my own father, I had found myself *really* turned around. So turned around I might as well have been staring at my own fucking ass.

"You're always welcome here, Rex." Mia gave me a warm rub between the shoulders before going back to drying the cups.

In through the doggy door bolted Penelope, the golden retriever, with Tammy bouncing close behind her, nipping playfully at the golden's tail. When Tammy realized I was in the room, she came straight to me, cheerily chirping and standing up on her hind legs, the entire length of her long body reaching up to my thigh.

"It's incredible to me how well she remembers you," Mia said, watching as I gave my favorite otter some head scratches. Benji watched, too, a thin smile on his lips.

This sucked. Not the otter pets, but the awkward energy that simmered between the two of us. I hated it as much as I hated the situation I found myself in. Benji had too nice of a smile to keep hidden.

"I remember when you guys had just gotten her. She could fit in the palm of my hand."

"Yup," Mia said. "And you'd always come over to bottle-feed her. I think Mav started getting jealous at one point."

"He did once say I hung out with Tammy more than him."

Benji cleared his throat. "All right, I'm headed to bed."

Mia shot a glance at the clock hanging on the wall. "It's only eight. Are you feeling sick?"

"No," Benji said, shrugging. He didn't offer anything else. He placed the last of the dishes he had been drying into the cabinet and headed out of the kitchen, leaving a trail of questions in his wake.

I asked the first one I could pull from the murk. "Is he okay?"

Mia shook her head, placing both hands on the countertop, the reds of her freshly painted nails popping against the white quartz. She looked out the window above the sink, at the setting sun that dipped below the tree line.

"I... I don't know."

"How long has he been acting like this?"

Mia seemed to do some calculating before saying,

"Since he came home over the summer. He lost his job and was having trouble finding another one, so we told him to come home and regroup. Since then, he's just been looking so beat down." Mia dropped her head, and I could see how much she'd been thinking about it. Her shoulders slumped. "I've asked him what's wrong, and he won't open up. But I see it, same as you did, Rex. I just don't know what to do about it."

I wanted to reassure her somehow, but I felt at a similar loss. Probably even more than she did. If she couldn't get through to him, there'd be no way that he'd listen to me.

Fuck... What if I'm making it worse for him just by being here?

The thought hit me like a hammer over the head. It was a thought I hated. There'd been a time when we had both helped each other immensely, and now, all that felt like it had happened three lifetimes ago. This Benji was so vastly different from the one who I kissed under the Costa Rican canopy. He'd been the first kiss I ever had with another guy, and it unlocked a piece of me that I had hoped would suffocate inside before ever seeing the light of day.

Benji helped me in not only accepting my body, but also my sexuality.

And now, instead of helping him, I was possibly hurting him.

"He'll be okay," Mia said, rolling her head so that her chin reached her chest, her neck popping. "He's my little Benj, he'll be okay."

"He will."

Mia's phone vibrated against the counter, her cheery ringtone dinging through the kitchen. She grabbed it, and her eyes went wide as she read whatever appeared on her screen. I wrapped things up with the dishes, squeezing the water from the sponge and washing the soap suds down the drain.

"I can't believe it," Mia said. "It's from the adoption agency." She looked like she was about to start jumping up and down. "Oh, I have to call Ashley. I can't believe it! They're moving us into the final step for the adoption."

"That's great!" She wrapped me in one of those hugs that could only follow a bout of incredible news. Mav had filled me in on the rocky process his moms had been having with the adoption of a boy named River. He was fostered by one of their volunteers, who unfortunately couldn't care for him much longer, and instead of letting him bounce to another foster home, Mia and Ashley had started the process of adopting him. It had been stalled by a development that scared everyone involved: an obsessive stalker by the name of "the Dove," who had been demanding that the Gold Sanctuary be shut down. From what Mav told me, the psycho had made multiple threats and had almost driven Mia and Ashley into picking up and moving, leaving their little paradise of an animal sanctuary in Georgia and going somewhere extremely far and way more safe.

Thankfully, they didn't have to do any of that. The Dove had been caught. About a month ago, cameras picked up on the man who tried sneaking onto the sanctuary late at night. He had a dove tattooed on his shoulder and had been spitting all kinds of crazy conspiracies as the police were cuffing him, about how the animals were being used for government testing and that there was a nuclear base underneath the horse stables.

Mia was already calling Ashley on FaceTime, her smile reaching from ear to ear. I thought I'd leave the two alone, so I congratulated her one more time before I stepped out.

I walked down the hall and into the living room, where Kaitlyn lay asleep with a book on her chest and Chester the calico sleeping by her feet. Next to the couch was a baby pen, where three baby raccoons rolled around with each other. I tried not to wake Kaitlyn as I crossed the living room, silently opening the door leading to the outside.

A Georgia fall felt much nicer than those in New York, soooo, silver lining, I guess? I could wear shorts and a shirt like I did now and not worry about freezing my balls right off.

The guesthouse was sandwiched between the pool and the reptile house. Usually, I cut through the back-yard since that was the quickest and most direct way to get there. Tonight, an unfamiliar tug made me take the longer route, taking a left and going back inside the house, through a guest bathroom. I walked out into another hall, this one lined with family photos. Some of them included me smiling alongside the Golds. One of the photos, framed inside a thin gold frame, made me pause, a smile overtaking my face.

A picture from our trip to Costa Rica. Benji and I stood next to each other, and although I was dead sure we weren't, it sure as hell looked like the two of us were holding hands.

Something I wanted to do so fucking bad. I knew by then that I was bi, and that I wanted Benji more than anything in the damn world. More than anyone else, all I wanted was Benji. But it felt wrong, on so many different fronts. First off, being the closeted son of a high-profile conservative politician didn't make it easy. Having a stepmom who'd founded one of the leading anti-queer organizations hellbent on keeping families 'normal' (whatever the fuck normal even meant) *certainly* didn't make what I was feeling any easier to accept.

But then there was the fact that Benji was my best friend's little brother. It was an unwritten rule, but it was a rule. I didn't want to break it. I risked losing not only my best friend but also my found family, a group of people who took me in and loved and cared for me more than my own flesh and blood did.

And yet... it was Benjamin Gold, the one whose kiss stole my breath, who stole so much more than my breath...

The light in his room was on. It was the last door in the hall, before making the turn that led out to the guesthouse. There was no sound coming from behind the door, but I figured he was in there.

I could leave him alone. Maybe that would be the better option, for the both of us.

Truth was, as much as I'd been trying to avoid Benji, I had instead found myself searching for him every chance I could get. I wanted to talk to him. I needed us to get back to what we had been, back when the world felt like a limitless playground and time would for sure stretch on into infinity.

Back when I didn't have to worry about a sex tape leaking.

The thought made my pulse instantly shoot up. Goose pimples broke out in a rampage down my neck and arms.

I could go and fester inside the guest bedroom,

thinking about all the shit swirling around my head. I didn't need to knock on Benji's door. Hell, maybe it wasn't smart of me to even knock in the first place.

I could...

My knuckles rapped on the bedroom door. There wasn't even a choice, right or wrong. There was only one thing: making sure Benji was good. That's all that mattered.

I heard movement from the other side of the door. Bedsheets rustling and a mattress squeaking. Footsteps followed next. The door lock clicked open, and Benji's head appeared in the crack, backlit by a lamp on his nightstand. He was already in a pair of sleeping shorts and a gray tank top, his glasses on and socks off.

"Sorry, I just... well, you kind of left the kitchen looking pretty beat down... I'm just going to ask you right out: Are you doing all right?"

Benji's brows rose in surprise, and the door opened a little wider. "I, um, yeah, I'm fine." His gaze dropped down to his bare feet, his toes digging into the thick carpet. "Thanks for checking in."

"All right... and you're sure?"

"I'm sure."

Something in Benji's demeanor told me otherwise.

"Want to go for a walk?" I asked.

"Huh?"

"I know it's late, but walking and getting some

fresh air always helps me out. We can take a little midnight walk through the sanctuary." It wasn't midnight, not for another three hours or so, but still, maybe he'd recall that special midnight we shared back in Costa Rica.

That velvet midnight I would never be able to forget, and one I'd never want to forget either.

His head lifted, eyes meeting mine. The growing smile on his face told me he remembered. But the smile was only a flash, as brief as a street-side firework. In moments, Benji deflated again.

"I'm good, Rex. Thanks." He started to close the door.

Fuck. He's not good. And I didn't want to leave him. I felt like if we could just talk things through underneath the stars, then maybe Benji could start feeling better. I didn't think he'd be back to 100 by sunup, but still, I didn't like the idea of him going back behind a locked door so he could sit in the swamp of his emotions.

"Benji, just a quick walk. We can go up to the lake and come right back."

He stalled in closing the door, and for a second, I thought I did it. He appeared to make a move for the shoes on the floor.

Instead, he shook his head and closed the door, the

lock clicking back into place after I heard a murmured "good night."

The hallway felt empty, even with all the warm memories that hung up on the white walls. The walk outside to the guesthouse wasn't as soothing as I had sold to Benji. In fact, the fresh air did jack shit to help the anxious thoughts from barreling into the forefront of my brain.

And the biggest one of those thoughts? It wasn't about my dad or the sex tape or the blackmail. It was about Benji.

What if I'm making him feel worse? Just by being here?

The thought careened through my head like a rocket ship breaking through an atmosphere, a fiery cannonball of chaos.

All night, it was all I could think about. Sometime around three in the morning was when I decided two things:

One. I'd find a way to leave by the weekend. Benji didn't need me around, as badly as I was beginning to want it.

Two. I needed a glass of water and a heavy dosage of melatonin.

7

BENJAMIN GOLD

I ROLLED over on the bed, my iPad almost falling off. I caught it before it fell face-first off the cliff of my twin-sized platform bed. My moms had offered to upgrade it to a full, but something about the smaller bed kept me comfortable. It always felt weird going to hotels and getting all this extra space to move around in.

Back when I felt things. The good ol' days, when emotions and thrills and fears and hopes didn't roll off me like I was coated in an oil slick.

The clock on the nightstand seared the time into my head with the bright red numbers: three in the morning.

I reached for my water bottle, sighing the second I lifted the empty bottle. My throat protested the development with a dry cough. I debated just staying in bed and ignoring the parchment paper that seemed to be clogging my esophagus. The thought of throwing off my sheets and walking the entire thirty feet or so it took to get to the kitchen gave me the chills.

But I'm soooo thirsty.

Ugh. Fine.

Sheets off, door open, floor creaking. I tiptoed down the dark hallway, hoping I didn't wake up any of the animals. Penelope was a super-light sleeper, and Tammy turned into a wereotter if someone interrupted her beauty sleep. If you've never heard an otter hiss bloody murder, then accidentally wake her up and get ready to cover your ears.

I dodged the spots in the floor I knew would creak the loudest. I could have gotten to the kitchen with my eyes closed at this point. I hadn't been expecting to be back home at the age of twenty-four, when everyone else seemed to be kick-starting their lives and careers, but hey, at least I was comfortable. It felt good, like being back in the womb somehow. The low ceilings and chips in the paint were comforting to me, carrying memories of being a kid, running through the halls with my siblings and feeling an overwhelming sense of love and happiness.

Yup. Those really were the good days.

I made it through the hall and past the living room without waking anyone or thing up. I almost forgot about the baby raccoons, but being nocturnal meant I also didn't have to worry about them; they were already making their tiny little baby raccoon noises from inside the pen.

Inside the kitchen, I went straight for the fridge, not even bothering with the light. There was plenty of moonlight coming in from the window anyway. I filled up my water bottle and took an icy-cold sip, my body immediately thanking me with a satisfied and involuntary "ahh."

"Can't sleep?"

"What the—!"

I didn't drop my water bottle by a miracle of divine making. It would have sounded like a nuclear bomb went off.

"Rex, jeez, you scared me."

"Sorry, should have turned on the light."

"Do you usually hang out in dark kitchens at the dead of night? Or is this a special occasion?"

My heart raced as my vision adjusted to the dim lighting. Rex leaned against the island, a glass of water in his hand. He wasn't wearing a shirt, which made my heart pound even harder. I thought I could make out the dark shape of a tattoo on his chest, underneath the hair, but I didn't want to stare (or lose control and dive headfirst).

"Special occasion," Rex said. He took a sip of his water and set the glass down, ice clinking together. "It's my last night here."

I reeled back a little, confused and surprised. "You didn't say you were leaving."

"I didn't know I was until a few hours ago."

I reached behind me and flipped the light switch. This had to be a joke, and I had to see Rex's face to determine that. It took a minute for my eyes to stop shutting at the sudden light, but he didn't seem like he was joking. His face seemed serious, set in the decision. His lips were turned down into a sad smirk.

My eyes flitted down. Only a moment, but *fuck*, now I could clearly see the tattoo on his chest, and I could see a clear trail of hair for me to kiss my way down, licking and sucking while he slipped out of those blue gym shorts. I wanted to rub him up and down, feeling that big body under my hands, tasting him and—

I turned the light back off.

"It was too bright," I said. "So what happened?"

How was it that even with the lights off, Rex still had the brightest blue eyes under the sun?

"A lot happened," Rex answered. Now he was the one

dodging things. Was he paying me back for shutting the door on him earlier? I really did appreciate that moment, way more than I was able to put into words. Even though I could still remember the text he sent, ending any and all hope of us ever being together, I still felt a warmth fill me when I heard Rex's voice on the other side of my door.

And now he's leaving. Great. Just like old times.

"Where are you going?" I didn't want to let up. Part of me felt a spark of something—anger? Confusion?

Fear?

Whatever it was, I wanted to keep feeling it. It had been so long...

"I've got a friend in Tampa—I can crash on her couch for a little. Lay low until this tape situation gets unfucked. Maybe while that happens, I'll hit the books again. Reapplying to law school is on the table."

"Really?" I said, wanting to smile and cry at the same time. I'd been such a blank slate of emotions that this sudden tug-of-war inside my chest made either one feel extreme.

"We'll see. First priority is getting out of your hair."

"Out of my hair? What's that mean?"

"As in leaving your proxi—"

"Rex, I know what the *phrase* means. I'm asking why do you think you have to 'get out of my hair'?"

"Because it's obvious you don't want me here, and I

don't think I blame you. I hate having these dreams of you smiling and then seeing you shut up in your bedroom all day, avoiding eye contact whenever you do come out. I don't want to make you feel uncomfortable or upset, so if I have to go, then I'm going to go."

I turned the light back on.

"Whoa, whoa, okay, I don't know where all this is coming from—"

"From the fact that this is the longest conversation we've had since I got here. I can tell there's friction between us, and I fucking hate it."

I huffed. "That's true." And then I put a hand on my face. "Ugh, I'm sorry, Rex. I've been going through it, all right, and none of 'it' has to do with you—" *Not entirely true, but...* "It's more with me, and how defeated I've been feeling."

"Defeated about what?"

A shrug was all I could really offer. I didn't want to talk about it, not now. Maybe not ever. But definitely not now.

"Benj, talk to me. Forget about everything for a second and just be here, with me. Talk to me. Tell me what you're feeling."

Nothing. I wanted to shout that I was feeling nothing, and that felt like the scariest thing in the entire world. Motivation ran out of me like a broken faucet, every day getting worse.

"I'm feeling... not great." I didn't want to talk about it. Didn't have the energy to. "But it's fine," I said, trying my best to brush it off, wishing the lights were off again so Rex couldn't look into my eyes. "But now that you know it's got nothing to do with you, are you still gonna head out?"

I tried to make the question sound as casual as possible, as if I didn't care either way, but the way Rex looked at me, with a half-cocked grin, told me I didn't do a great job.

"Well... My main reason was leaving to make you feel better, but if that won't be the case—"

"It won't."

"Then yeah, I'll stay. I'd have an easier time studying by the lake than in my friend's living room anyway."

"I can help out, too. If you want my help."

Rex chuckled. "Of course I'd want your help."

More of that same warmth from earlier, flooding through me. It was very different from the cold anxiety I'd been doused with when Rex first arrived, when all I could see of him was that damn text. The one seared into my head like a paragraphs-long burning brand.

"Benjamin, we can't ever speak about what we've done, and we can't ever do it again. You were a mistake, and now that it's out of my system, it's done. Never again."

That was on the last day of our trip to Costa Rica. I had cried for hours on the plane ride home, burying my face in a pillow and pretending I had gone straight to sleep. Rex had never spoken to me after that, not until two weeks ago when he'd shown up at the sanctuary like a bear needing rescue.

"Since we're being so talkative..." This was me dipping my toe in potential murky waters, but still, I had to know. "What happened between you and your dad? Why did you leave everything in New York for our little sanctuary in Georgia?"

Rex cracked his neck. He didn't say anything at first, making me worried that I might have overstepped some invisible boundary.

"My dad, he's running for re-election this year. It's probably the worst time ever for his only son to be involved in a sex scandal."

"In a *what*?" I must not have heard right. Rex, although definitely not the most vanilla guy around, didn't seem like someone who'd get wrapped up in a salacious scandal. Even in Costa Rica, he had been extra careful about us kissing and hooking up.

"Benji, since our trip, since that one night we spent together, I've known one thing for sure: I'm not straight. I'm bi, a hundred percent. I love dick way too much to be straight. But no matter how sure I felt, I could *never* be open about it. So when I hooked up with this girl, Penelope, who told me she loves to watch two guys go at it, I asked if she'd help, uh, facilitate this. We'd hook up, the three of us, at least once a month, sometimes more. I trusted them. It wasn't some random people I met through an app, so I felt safe. I let my guard down."

"Crap."

"Yeah. Crap." He rubbed a hand over his mouth, stress lines forming on his forehead. "Last week, I was at a party with Mav. I was hooking up with Penelope and Scott, and that's when I saw the hidden camera."

I gasped, my heart sinking and my stomach twisting into a tight knot. "Are you fucking joking? What happened?"

"I grabbed the camera and threw it against the wall. But it was too late—whatever they got was streamed up into the cloud or whatever." He lifted a weak hand up toward the ceiling. "They sent an email to my dad before I had even left the party. They threatened to leak the video if he didn't send a hundred thousand dollars."

"Rex... My God."

"My dad didn't send any money—I wouldn't have wanted him to. But he did cut me off immediately, and seeing as how I wasn't exactly being frugal up until then, I didn't have anything saved. Your brother offering me the guesthouse was a lifeline I'll never forget."

"I can't believe it... Do you have any idea of who has the tape?"

"None. Mav helped hire a private investigator, who's looking into it for me, but I'm not all that hopeful. I feel like they're either waiting for the hundred thousand or waiting for the week before voting starts to dominate the news cycle."

I winced. This physically hurt me. The invasion of privacy and loss of control made me sick.

"I'm sure the detective will find that tape before it leaks. Mav has good judgment—I'm sure he got the best detective he could find."

"Maverick did sound pretty excited by him." He let out a breath that sounded like he'd been holding it for years. "I don't know. We'll see, I guess. I try not to think about it too much." His frown started to grow into a smile. "I'm glad I don't have to leave either. You're a great distraction. I'm only obsessing over my problems for about half the day; the other half I'm thinking about you."

That brought a blush to my cheeks. The heat spread through me, lighting up parts that *shouldn't* be lit right then.

"I'm glad you're staying, too," I said.

"Well, good," Rex said, a hand running absentmindedly over his chest, seemingly unaware of the effect that move had on me.

He's about to be very aware if he looks down.

"I didn't want to leave so soon. I've missed you, Benji."

Oh. Okay, wasn't expecting all that.

"I missed you, too."

It's done. Never again.

"You know, Benj, ever since that trip to Costa Rica, I've... I don't know. Everywhere I go, I feel like I'm looking for something. Someone." Rex took in a breath, his hand falling to his side. "When I got here, I didn't feel like that anymore. Even though my entire life is turned upside down, something about being around you made things start feeling right again. Even if we were in separate rooms or if we were right next to each other. Something about knowing you were good and only a door's knock away, it makes things feel okay."

I swallowed what felt like a boulder. "That trip..."

"It changed my life, Benji. You changed my life."

"But... fuck, Rex. I don't mean to be dramatic but... well, you kind of ruined mine."

His eyes opened wide at that. He looked like a fish out of water, mouthing some words that didn't add up well enough to form a proper sentence.

"You did," I said. I'd already opened the wound, might as well address it fully.

"Okay, I think it's time we talked about Costa Rica, then," Rex said, crossing his arms, biceps looking good enough to take a bite out of.

Focus.

And not on those thick thighs or big arms.

"Fine," I said, ready to open this can of galaxy-sized worms. "Let's talk about it."

8

REX MADISON

SIX YEARS AGO

THE PLANE'S engine started up, rumbling the aircraft with its powerful vibrations. I was sitting next to Mav, talking about what we'd do when we got back home. I didn't want to leave—this trip had been incredible on so many fucking levels.

"I think I'm going to move to New York," Mav said over the engines.

"Really?"

"Yeah, man, I need to spread my wings a little. Come with me. Your dad's election is this year, shit's going to get crazy. Just come up to the city with me."

It sounded like a good plan, but... I looked over to the two rows ahead of us. Benji sat with his head already buried in a pillow, which was weird considering he normally was scared of flying.

We talked all weekend, just us two, about the kind

of things we'd do together in Georgia. I promised him I'd come out. I even texted it to him that same morning, like I wanted to get it down on paper or something. I told him I'd talk to Mav, and that he'd understand. Maybe he'd be upset for a few days, a week max, but he'd come around. He'd realize what we both did; there was an undeniable fit between the two of us. We went together like salt and pepper, sun and star, air and wind.

Fucking hell, he was making me all Shakespeare over him.

"I don't know, man," I said. "I think I'm going to stay."

"Shit, really?" Maverick's eyebrows knit together. "You sure? Do you have a fever or something?"

It's a fever all right.

"Yeah, I'm sure," I said, picturing my time with Benji from here on out.

"Damn, all right. Well, I'm officially shocked. Bamboozled." Maverick sat back in his seat, the plane dipping as we approached our landing.

SHOCKED.

Fucking shocked.

How had I been the one to ruin Benji's life? After I was the one who had been ghosted, set aside like a torn bag of rancid trash, thrown away as quickly as a piece of dog crap.

Heat rushed to my cheeks. At least he wanted to talk about it. Good, I'd be able to bring up exactly what I was feeling, and Benji would be able to address it head-on. No more of this festering under the surface shit.

"I thought everything was good between us, Benj. I sat on that plane ride home daydreaming about what a future with you would look like. I initially turned down Maverick's plan to move with him. And then the plane landed, I go to talk to you and you flip."

"I flip?" Benji seemed surprised.

"Yes." I went full steam ahead, unloading the six years of pent-up emotions I had stored since that day. "I went to talk to you, I went to go tell you how fucking excited I was about things. I was going to show you the message I wrote to my dad. And then you started yelling at me, pushing me away. In front of everyone."

"I'm in the twilight zone. This is the Upside Down, isn't it?"

Benji's confusion only worked to make me confused, dissipating some of the boiling frustration. "Are you saying you never went off on me?"

"No, I remember very clearly going off on you, but you're acting as if I didn't have a reason."

"A reason? We had spent the entire night together, and like six nights before that."

He shook his head. The light of the kitchen bounced off his light amber eyes. There was a quick flash of self-consciousness in that I wasn't wearing a shirt, standing in Benji's kitchen with my stomach out and a hand on my bare chest. I thought everyone would be knocked out at this time.

The thoughts of self-consciousness drifted away. This was Benji standing in front of me. The one who taught me to be okay with my body in the first place. He had shown me how to love myself, and he had done it with a hungry look in his eyes. I had a feeling I could be sans shirt *and* shorts and still be okay in front of him.

A very strong feeling.

"Rex," Benji said, sounding exhausted. "If you're just going to ignore it, then I might as well bring it up."

"Ignore what?" I wanted to shout. Not at Benji, but at the situation that fucked us up to begin with. What could have been bad enough to have caused a six-year-long rift? I thought it had been Benji's choice, thought he might have just gotten a frigid case of cold feet.

Benji grabbed his phone and started scrolling, flicking his finger down the screen, a blur of photos moving with his swipes. My brows knit together. I waited for him to find whatever he was looking for, having zero fucking idea of what it could possibly be.

"One second," he said. "It's been a while. I know I screenshotted it... Here."

He handed me the phone. It was a screenshot of a text conversation, my name at the top of the window. It started with me saying how excited I was and how happy Benji made me. I remembered typing that out, after a particularly explosive night. I'd been floating on cloud nine all day, smiling even though I was in charge of cleaning dung off the floor that day.

I kept reading, my smile quickly fading. Underneath Benji's reply to my text with a bunch of smiley faces and stars, there was another text. It said it was from me, but I didn't recognize it. Not one word of it.

"Benjamin, we can't ever speak about what we've done, and we can't ever do it again. You were a mistake, and now that it's out of my system, it's done. Never again."

I read the words out loud, mostly to myself, none of it making sense.

"I never... what the hell? Benjamin? Since when do I ever call you Benjamin?"

"I dunno, I thought that was just you trying to be formal." He arched a brow, his arms crossed against his chest. "But calling me a mistake? I think I'd take my full name over that."

"No, no, this isn't—"

"Why? Everything was going so well. I... we... You were my first time, Rex. I fell hard for you."

Another explosive reveal. "First? I was your first? But you said—"

"Yeah, I lied. I wanted to impress you."

I set the phone down on the counter, pointing at it. "Benj, I never wrote that. Not a single word of that text came from me. I would never have sent that. I would never have even thought that."

He cocked his head. I could tell he searched for the truth, the way his gaze bounced across my face. There was nothing to hide, no twitches to give me away.

It was the truth. "I didn't send that text."

"I mean, I didn't photoshop it if that's what you're saying."

"Of course that's not what I'm saying. I don't know what happened. Maybe someone in Costa Rica stole my phone, sent that text without me knowing. But I swear, Benji. On everything I've got. It wasn't me."

He bit his lip. Chewed it pink. "Really?"

"I swear. That wasn't me." I rubbed the back of my head, shocked at how this night began to unfold. "So all this time, six fucking years, all because of that?" I wanted to shout and laugh and cry, all at once.

"But then..."

"Who sent it?"

He nodded, shooting a worried glance at the phone. Did he trust me? How else could I prove it to him?

"I'll figure that out," I said. "I want to know as bad as you do. I can't fucking believe it. Six years. I moved out of the state, thinking I'd be better off. Instead, I climbed deeper in the closet and ended up with an involuntary sex tape hanging over my head." The room felt colder, even though the heater was blasting a wave of warm air in our direction.

"Meanwhile, I was wishing I just up and left to New York, thinking that I'd bump into you on the subway or at a coffee shop. I daydreamed about that pretty much twenty-four seven, after the initial anger over that text wore off." His lips curled into a smile. "No matter what, I really couldn't stop thinking about you."

"Fuck," I said again, but this time my smile matched Benji's. "'Benjamin.' Who even calls you that?"

"No one. Absolutely no one, except maybe at the DMV."

A laugh from the both of us seemed to warm the room up again, anxiety and questions drifting away, leaving only me and Benji, standing a few feet apart, so close I could practically feel his body heat on me.

Or was that my own? Rising up like a thermostat left under a blazing sun.

Benji looked at me, his smile slanting back down. "I'm sorry," he said, his gaze dropping to the floor. "I shouldn't have blown up on you. If I just talked with you about it, we could have figured it out."

"No, don't do that." Without thinking, I put a finger under his chin and brought his eyes back up to mine. "We can't live in the 'what-ifs' like that. Shit happened, it was unfortunate, but it's history now. We have to take it, learn from it, and create an even brighter future from it. Who knows, maybe if we had stayed together, things would have somehow turned out a thousand times worse. Maybe we needed those six years apart so we could appreciate every single second that comes after."

My hand, at some point, moved from his chin to the back of his neck. I rubbed soft circles with my thumb.

Benji didn't answer me, not with words at least. Instead, he pushed upward, his hands falling on my chest, and, in one breathless motion, he kissed me.

It felt like a super-cut from the creation of the galaxy zooming in on the two of us little souls locking lips, pressing our bodies against each other like we were desperate to become one. His tongue probed and licked and swirled, dancing with mine. His hands made circles around my bare chest, and our gym shorts did absolutely nothing to hide either of our excitement.

And then I remembered. We were still in his moms' kitchen, not exactly an ideal place for this rigid reunion.

"Let's move this to the guesthouse," I said, growling against his lips. He smiled and kissed me, both of our cocks throbbing between us.

"Let's."

He turned off the light and started out the kitchen door. It was much colder outside than in, but with Benji holding my hand, I felt like I could dive into a pool of ice water and be completely fine.

We walked across the dark path that led around the pool and toward the guesthouse, where the light from the living room shone through the drawn blinds. I couldn't get him inside fast enough, already feeling a tightening in my core.

"Whoa, hold up a sec." Seemed like Benji had slightly different plans. He stopped us before we got into the guesthouse, only a few steps away.

"Looks like Tarrek didn't close the volunteer gate before he left."

Tarrek Sarnihov was one of the new volunteers Mia had brought on to the sanctuary, and I remembered him because he had a little bit of an attitude when we first got introduced. I thought he seemed an odd fit at the Gold sanctuary, with his biker gang–like demeanor and take-no-shit-from-anyone attitude, but one thing about Mia and Ashley was that they never judged any book by their cover.

If he can't even close a gate right, maybe it's time to shelve him.

It was a bitter thought, and only came because I was in a hurry to get Benji behind closed doors and completely butt-ass naked, and this whole "gate being open" detour was taking at least fifteen seconds away from butt-ass-naked time.

Six years is long enough.

Benji came back onto the path, grinning with a devilish look in his eyes as he looked down at my bulging shorts.

"All done," he said.

"Great, now we can get started, then."

I led Benji to the guesthouse, every footstep making my heart beat that much faster, my shorts feel that much tighter. There was a growing and unanchored need for him inside my gut, growing up from my groin, taking over my entire body like a wind-driven blaze.

The second we made it into the guesthouse, all bets were off. I turned to him, met with a gaze that shouted with lust. He bit his lower lip, and I didn't even have to ask, not like all those years ago. I already knew the answer. I could feel it, the way our shorts both bulged. He was close enough for me to feel the heat, the stiffness. I could feel him throb against me, matching my own desperate pulse.

His hands landed on my chest as he looked up into my eyes, his lips turned into that smile I had so fucking missed.

I couldn't take it. I needed his lips against mine. I leaned down, locking us together, his wet lips parting for my tongue, needy and hungry. The taste of Benji on my tongue filled me with an insatiable thirst. He was everything I'd been missing. This kiss caught us up on the six years we'd been apart and tied together all our past lives in one quick swoop of the tongue.

He moaned, a sound that made my cock throb between us. I felt the sticky warmth of my precome leak onto my thigh.

"God, I fucking missed this."

"I can't believe it took us six years."

"I'm going to make up for every fucking second."

Benji grinned at me as my hand went down to cup his bulge. "You better."

Our lips locked again. I pushed my hips forward, pushing us toward the couch. I didn't even bother with the lights, not wanting to pry myself off Benji for even a second. I kissed him as I cupped his head in my hands. He ground his hard length against mine, and it was my turn to moan, the delicious pressure making me see stars even through my shut eyes.

"Sit down," I said, half command and half plea.

Benji did, his shorts tented and twitching. I licked my lips and dropped my shorts, letting the moonlight shine off the precome that leaked from my tip. Benji's eyes opened wide, and his jaw parted.

"Damn" was all he said as he started to move forward.

"No." I pushed him back on the couch. "Not yet." I went down on my knees, my mouth watering for the sight in front of me.

Benji's surprise turned into a grin as I started to pull off his shorts. He lifted off the couch, and I gave one last pull.

His hard dick flopped out, making a loud slapping sound. He still had his shirt on, but I could see the muscles of his six-pack already showing.

I moved in, licking my lips and making sure I was soaking wet as I sucked Benji into my mouth. Without using hands, I took him between my lips and licked, tasting his salty precome and instantly wanting more. I ran my tongue across his slit, making his body shake underneath me, his head falling back on the couch. His hands came up to grab fistfuls of hair as my tongue swirled around him.

"Oh fuck," he hissed, thrusting his hips upward.

He took off his shirt and tossed it to the side, revealing a body of lines and muscles I wanted to spend a lifetime memorizing.

I swallowed more of him down my throat, thankful that my gag reflexes never seemed to develop, because *fuck* did Benji have a tonsil-tickling-sized cock.

And I fucking loved it.

"That's it, Rex, fuck, that feels so good."

It was like tossing a gallon of gasoline into a bonfire. I bobbed up and down on his dick, making sure it was sloppy, making sure I let him know just how fucking bad I wanted him. With one hand I played with his tight balls, and with the other I jerked myself off, feeling pleasure in every sense of the word.

I pulled off his cock and looked up at him, rubbing the head of him across my lips. The drunk grin he gave me only pushed me further. I slapped myself with his dick, hard against my cheek. He bit his lip, the pink skin going momentarily pale. I collected a glob of spit before letting it loose on his rock-hard cock. The foamy white spit rolled off the head, down his shaft.

I rubbed, up and down, the slick sounds of wet skin filling the room. I spit into my other hand and used it to get my dick wet. We both started to grunt, moan, eyes rolling back, balls tightening, chest flushing. I kept jerking us off, keeping a momentum.

Benji's hands reached out to either side of him on the couch. "Oh God, Rex. Fuck, I'm so close."

I was too. So close I couldn't even warn him. I stood up before the wave crashed over me, giving me enough time to spray Benji with my come. It pooled on his chest as I twitched and spasmed, shot after shot.

"Oh fuck, fuck, yesss," Benji said, his word raising into a guttural grunt as he began shooting his load, adding to the mess of come on his chest and stomach.

It took us a moment for us to catch our breaths.

By then, the world stopped spinning and my body felt spent, every muscle relaxed, as if I'd been pumped with clouds.

"I, um," Benji said, looking down at the puddles of come dripping down the ridges of his six-pack. "I think I need a towel."

"No, you're going to need a whole-ass car wash to get that mess off you."

Laughter filled the guesthouse as I went to go grab him a towel.

Everything, for the first time in a very long time, began to feel *right*.

9

BENJAMIN GOLD

LAST NIGHT MADE me feel alive again, something I hadn't really felt in years. Sure, that could sound dramatic to some people, but to me, it was just the simple truth. I hadn't felt that kind of euphoric rush or brain-melting release of endorphins since the time I'd dated a guy in college who knew how to tie an entire cherry stem army with his tongue.

And the postorgasmic bliss that followed reminded me that the rush wasn't just from the incredible sex I had, but it was also about *who* I had it with.

Rex Madison, the one and only. My first crush and my last love. I'd never say that out loud, but I had admitted it to myself long before, on a night I had two entire bottles of red wine.

That's the night I admitted it to myself: I had fallen

in love with Rex underneath the star-blanketed sky of Costa Rica.

I considered staying the rest of the hours left until sunrise. Considered cuddling up with Rex in the bed, going for round two and three and four.

Most of all, I didn't want the night to end. I didn't want the emptiness, the gaping numbness, to return. I wanted to keep this bubbly happiness and giddy excitement. I wanted to hold on to the intoxicating arousal, the fire-in-your-chest anticipation. Even the anger turned confusion turned relief at the revelation that Rex had never been the one to send that text message.

I wanted to keep it all, *feel* it all.

Instead, I turned down his offer of moving to the bed. I toweled off and kissed him again before saying good night and leaving to my bedroom.

Falling asleep was easy. The dreams that followed gave me wings that sent me straight through the clouds, into the stars.

Morning brought the malicious numbness with it. Although I still felt the spots where Rex's lips kissed, where his tongue licked, and I could still smell his manly scent in my nose... it didn't bring back the torrent of emotions from last night. It didn't really bring back anything. I got out of bed, brushed my teeth, looked in the mirror, and I started to cry.

It was soft at first, the crying that you think you

might be able to control. More for dramatic effect than anything else.

That was only the precursor to the storm. Tears started to flow harder as, the longer I looked in the mirror, the less I recognized the face staring back.

My eyes looked slightly sunken, and instead of smile lines, I could spot lines across my forehead and between my brow. My jaw, constantly tensed, seemed almost strained. I could never truly grow a beard, but the splotchy shadow of hair was trying its damned hardest. I needed a haircut, the dark brown strands starting to grow over my ears.

This wasn't me. This was never me.

I grew up as a solid stone of support, always able to roll with the punches life threw at us. Optimism was my drug. Even when it seemed like the world stacked everything against us, I kept on smiling and trying to hold on to the positive. When Dusty stopped talking to people for a year, I was there to help him back; I was there when I knew he wouldn't even mumble a word to me. I stuck by his side, and most importantly, I smiled and joked and tried to keep the light of life alive.

I don't know exactly when, or exactly why, or even exactly how, but I knew that my own light had gone out and I had no idea how to turn it back on.

I should be happy. I shouldn't be crying. I'm

healthy, I'm with family, Rex is back in my life. I should be happy.

I cried harder. I turned the faucets to full force, hoping it would drown out the sobs that were wrenched from my body.

I can't be happy. I can't.

At some point, I sank to the floor. The black-and-white tiles felt cold on my knees, my palms. I dropped my head in the cave my arms created.

I'm broken.

The thought rang in my head like a shattered bell, its chaotic sound making my head hurt. Or maybe that was the crying? Could be the crying.

I wasn't sure how long I stayed on the bathroom floor, thinking about everything: my lack of drive, the lack of any good prospects for a career, my lack of feeling any kind of elation for what happened last night.

At some point, the tears dried, and the water bill was most likely way higher than it should be. I stood and washed my face before turning off the water. The face reflected in the mirror looked like even more of a stranger, with puffy and red eyes. Still, somewhere underneath the sad mask, somewhere in there was the old Benji. I just needed to figure out how to pull him out.

The rest of the morning went by without

anymore spontaneous cry fests. I did start feeling a little better, as if the tears had helped remind me that I wasn't as broken as I liked to believe. The dark clouds in my head moved aside, and I started looking back at last night and feeling that same familiar spark light in my gut. I stayed in my room after my bathroom meltdown, but I decided to venture out around lunchtime. I'd been spending my lunches inside my room over the last few weeks, eating sandwiches and drinking protein shakes while I watched old anime episodes.

Not today. The sun hung bright and full in the sky, and the weather was that perfect Georgia mix of summer and fall. Not cold enough for coats and not hot enough for shorts. I threw on a T-shirt and some track pants, and I wandered outside, where my moms were hanging out by a table on the patio. Uncle Peanut was there, wearing a bright yellow and pink button-up shirt, the small amount of white hairs on his head trimmed short as if he were ready for a big date.

And Rex was there, too. He looked so damn good, and I wasn't just saying that because I'd seen him naked only about five hours earlier. No, even with clothes on, Rex looked like a man pulled right out of a "perfect guy" catalogue. He had a smile that glowed, and those sky-blue eyes of his matched the glow, flashes of last night streaking across my brain.

Flashes of those eyes, half-lidded and hungry, his mouth turned to an O as he blew his load all over me.

"Someone's looking spiffy," I said as I joined the four of them, focusing on Uncle Peanut and reminding myself that my moms were sitting only a few feet away from me.

Jack gave himself a vogue frame, working his haircut like a pro. "Aunt Gabbie cut it. She did a good job, right?"

"Damn, she did."

Mia covered her mouth and spoke in a stage whisper, "Don't tell him about the penis she shaved into the back of his head."

Ashley guffawed and Uncle Peanut laughed, too. Rex's laugh boomed. "Don't worry," he said. "I specially asked for that. I'm just upset she circumcised it—"

"All right, my mistake for going down this road," Mia said, dropping her head in her hands, cheeks flushing pink.

"You came at the perfect time," Ashley said, motioning at a chair. I sat, smiling. I may not have been feeling like myself lately, but my family never failed to bring me back down to earth.

I sat next to Rex, his oaky scent rushing into my nose. Under the table, like an instant magnetic pull, our knees pressed together.

"Ash is making lunch. You good with burgers and hotdogs?" my mom asked.

"Sounds good to me." And then I remembered something. "Hey, Ma," I said. "Last night, I was up late and I noticed the gate to the volunteer parking area was open. I closed it, but still, with everything that's gone on here, they should probably be on top of that."

Both my moms nodded, but Mia seemed more concerned than Ashley. She craned around in her chair, looking at the locked yellow gate that would have been impossible to climb over. Security around the Gold Sanctuary got real tight after we started getting threatened by someone named the Dove. They wanted to shut us down, although the reasons didn't seem very clear. My moms were convinced it was some animal rights person turned extremist, but I always had a sense that there was something more personal about it.

Either way, none of us were right. The Dove had been caught, and he was just some crazy lunatic, not attached to any animal rights groups or any past links in the family.

"I'll talk to them. We've got two new people; it might have been one of them," Mia said. "Cameras didn't pick up anything weird, so I doubt it's anything to worry about."

"Yeah, I'm sure it's fine." I settled into the chair, trying not to think too much about Rex's leg against mine. It brought with it a whole train of other thoughts: I want that leg on me, I want my face between his thighs, I want to stay up all day and night with him, talking, naked, loving, fucking.

I also wanted to figure out who sent that damn text.

"Do you think these are going to stay?" Ashley asked. "Tarrek seems a little out of it. And Bindy is scared of anything with teeth and also gags at the slightest smell of poop."

Uncle Peanut huffed. "Oh, she definitely won't be a good fit here, then."

"They'll be fine," Mia said. "The only volunteer who we've lost is Helena, and that's only because of family problems. I'm not running some kind of boot camp here."

"How is she?" I asked, realizing I hadn't seen her around in months. She'd been one of the first volunteers at the sanctuary and had become pretty close with the family. It was actually her foster child, River, who my parents were trying to adopt.

"She's doing all right. Some drama with her father, so she's had to go to Texas these last few months. River's with her, although now that this whole Dove situation is behind us, maybe we can bring him into the family and get him settled here before his sixteenth birthday."

Rex leaned back in his chair. "What a fucking

relief. Mav had been telling me about the threats that psycho left."

"It got scary," Ashley said, and we all nodded our agreement, a rogue chill traveling down my spine.

"There are some crazy-ass people out there," Rex said.

"Tell me about it," Uncle Peanut said, "I dated most of them."

It was the perfect opening. We fell into a long and elaborate and gut-busting sequence of stories that involved our Uncle Peanut and the various different conquests he'd had during his time as a famous celebrity photographer and beyond, living with Aunt Gabbie as an artist in the wine valley of California. My favorite story of his wasn't about the hilarious one-nighters he had or the disastrous blind dates he'd gone on.

Nah, my favorite story from Jack was about his first and true love, one that truly left his mark on Uncle Peanut's heart. His name was Ted, and he and Jack sounded like the perfect pair, only pulled apart by the tragic twists life sometimes brings, especially to those we think deserve them least.

Uncle Peanut was wrapping up a story about him and Ted, a story of them vacationing together in Peru, when my mom seemed to have been struck with a sudden thought.

"Sorry, Jack, it's just your story about scuba diving reminded me of something: Has anyone seen Tammy lately?" Mia asked, looking under the table. Normally she was chirping and bouncing around one of my moms' legs, if she wasn't a shadow behind Rex.

Rex shook his head. "I haven't seen her all day actually."

"That's weird." Ashley stood, looking around. The yard was large, and it connected to a few different buildings that all housed rehabilitated animals, along with the fields for the horses and the lake behind them. It wasn't unusual for Tammy to lounge by the lake; she was an otter after all.

I stood and Rex followed my lead. "Let's go check near the lake," I said. "She's probably diving around in there."

Rex and I left toward the lake as my parents and Uncle Peanut started to spread out across the yard, calling out for Tammy. Normally she came running at the first syllable of her name, so this did feel a little off. We walked down the stone path, looking into the bushes just in case she decided to take a nap. That was something she usually did in the summers, but on cooler days like today, she typically enjoyed them by the lake.

"So," Rex said, when we were out of sight from my moms. "About last night."

"Tammy! Yeah, about it. Tammy!"

"I really liked it. A whole fucking lot. Tammy!"

"So did I."

"Maybe we should head back to the guesthouse, after we find Tammy. Just, you know, to hang out."

I chuckled, trying to play things off as cool as I could. Meanwhile, I could feel my briefs getting tighter. "That sounds like a pla— Oh my God. Rex, look."

"Holy shit."

He saw it immediately. How could he not? It was a trail of dried blood, crusting against the leaves of green grass that led toward the quiet lake, its water serving as a reflective surface for the sun to bounce off. It took a few seconds for my eyes to adjust to the bright light, but when they did, my heart sank like a ship blown in two.

"Oh no, no, no." I spotted Tammy by the edge of the water and broke into a run. "Call for help!"

10

REX MADISON

TAMMY DIDN'T LOOK GOOD. She was extremely lethargic when we found her, barely able to lift her head up from the ground. A note hung loose around her neck, reading 'This won't end until the Golds do'. There was a cut on her front leg that must have been where the blood came from, and on her back, shaved into her fur, was the outline of a bird.

Except, we all knew it wasn't any kind of bird. Tammy's bare skin revealed the rough outline of a dove, with a line shaved at the beak to represent the olive branch. This was a message, and we'd received it loud and fucking clear.

Thankfully, the sanctuary had a vet station on-site. Benji picked Tammy up, and we ran. I called ahead, making sure Mia knew to tell the vet to rush.

"She'll be okay," I said as we ran, trying to reassure

both Benji and myself. We reached the small clinic and barreled through the doors. Mia hurried them into the exam room. I followed close behind, making sure I didn't get in the way but was still close enough to help.

"Is she breathing?" Mia asked.

Benji gently laid Tammy down on the exam table, swinging the light over her. "Barely. Her airways don't seem obstructed, and she's still conscious." Benji took a paw in his hand and gave her a small pinch. She jerked back. "She has feeling, so she's not paralyzed either."

If this wasn't such a scary moment, I would have stood back and admired Benji's shift in demeanor. He switched into leadership mode, taking the reins seemingly without a second thought. He walked around the table with confidence, the fear of the moment appearing to fuel his focus. He grabbed an oxygen mask from the rack and held it on Tammy's tiny snout, her eyes flitting open and closed.

"She had some nasal drip, and her muzzle looked wet, Mom."

Mia held up a syringe to the light, watching as the medication filled it to whatever mark she was looking for. She tapped out the air bubbles and felt around for the muscle in Tammy's thigh. Like a bee sting, she went in quick and efficient. Tammy didn't seem to notice a thing.

Benji worked with another needle, leaving the

oxygen mask resting on Tammy's snout. He pressed an alcohol wipe on her leg before feeling around with his thumb for a vein. Like a pro, he drew the blood before Tammy could even realize something was up.

"Run a full CBC."

"You got it."

"We'll see what Dr. Kenny says when he gets here —shouldn't be too long. But I think this is some kind of poison."

Benji nodded, filling a clear disc with the blood he had drawn before placing it in a diagnostic machine. "That's what I thought, too. Thankfully she didn't have enough to kill her."

"She's still not out of the woods yet," Mia said, tying her hair back in a ponytail and wiping the sweat from her forehead with the sleeve of her jacket.

Dr. Kenny arrived about five minutes later, rushing in with a stethoscope over his black golf polo. He thanked Benji and Mia, clearly impressed by how well they'd handled the triage. The results of the blood test were already being printed out, saving valuable time and showing Dr. Kenny that yes, Tammy had been poisoned. He got to work, neutralizing any of the poison that was left in her system while making sure she was stabilized.

Benji and I saw that neither of us could do much else for Tammy, not until she was feeling better.

"Mom, I'm going to go check out the security footage, see if we can spot whoever did this." Benji seemed much less shaken than when we initially stumbled on Tammy. He had gone a ghastly pale, making me think I'd be carrying them both to get help. That changed the second he stepped into the clinic and took the lead in saving Tammy's life.

"You did great in there," I said as we walked down the shaded path toward the house. The leaves looked like they were dipped in red and orange paint.

"I spent a lot of days hanging out in there."

"It showed." A thought struck me. "Why didn't you ever consider going to vet school?"

Benji pursed his lips in a thin smile. "I did at one point. School was just never my thing. Dusty got all the brains, and I got all the looks." He put a hand under his chin and cocked his head, laughing and sounding exactly like his identical twin.

"I don't believe that," I said, laughing with him, grateful that this moment allowed for laughter. It could have gotten real fucked-up if we hadn't found Tammy when we had.

"Why not look into it?" I asked, seeing a little bit of the spark in Benji's eyes, the one I recognized from when we were kids. He had always talked about doing big things, changing lives and being known, one way or another. He used to talk about being a commentator on

ESPN, or a famous sports doctor. He talked about opening up another sanctuary, and becoming a TV host for an animal conservation show. I remember him being fifteen and talking about going to Yale or Harvard. His dreams seemed endless, and it all appeared to be within Benji's reach.

Things had changed for him at some point, and his drive seemed to have sputtered, but I refused to believe it was too late for anything Benji wanted to accomplish.

"It's too late," he said.

"Not at all. Benj, you can do it. You graduated with a degree in Bio, didn't you? You probably need to take an exam, but we can study for that together. I'll work on my law school applications while we get you ready for vet school."

He seemed to chew on the thought, the silence encouraging me. It wasn't an outright "no," so that was good.

"I'll think about it," he said as we reached the house.

I wanted to push him harder, but after the shit we just went through, I felt his answer was more than good enough.

We crossed through the house, Penelope raising her golden head and sniffing at us before dropping it back down onto her bed which sat perfectly under two thick rays of sunlight. Benji pulled out a set of keys from his pocket and unlocked the security room, a tiny thing in the back of the first floor, next to the guest bathroom. It was windowless and lit up by a terrible fluorescent bulb that made it feel like we were walking into an old hospital room.

Benji took the lone seat in front of the computer, clicking in the password and opening up the security camera interface. I stood behind him, a hand on the chair. It was a small enough room that his head was next to my crotch, and it didn't look suspicious in the slightest—we were just crammed into the room.

Now, he if turned his head, then *that* would look suspicious.

Moments from last night flashed in my vision. As Benji looked for the recent footage, I couldn't help but think about how good last night felt. It went beyond hooking up. Last night had opened my eyes, and it lit a fire underneath my still-closeted ass.

I spent all morning thinking about it. Around lunchtime, before everything went down with Tammy, I had made a promise to myself: I was going to come out as bi. I'd make a public post and rip it off like a bandage. Let people run with the story however they'd want, I didn't care. I just wanted to be done with the hiding and the shame and the pressure of it all.

Plus, if the video ever did come out, it would take

some of the sting out. The headlines wouldn't read "Closeted Senator's Son Caught in a Sex Tape Scandal."

Still, it wouldn't take *all* the sting out... *What would Benji think?*

Fuck.

Anxiety took its throne inside my chest, holding each lung in either hand, squeezing. I took in a deep breath, trying to fight the pressure.

"All right, check it out," Benji said, holding a finger at the screen. I followed where he pointed, looking at the square of a black-and-white image. The timestamp in the corner said it was from the night before, at two in the morning.

Benji pressed Play and the trees unfroze, shifting in the wind, the moonlight highlighting the leaves and making it seem like a silver sea.

Underneath the ocean of silver leaves, something else flashed. A shape.

A person.

They wore a hefty coat, making it difficult to discern any kind of body type. A hat was pulled over their head, blocking the face. On the camera, the cap appeared to be white with two blue circles on the front, above the tongue. They moved in a hurry, going through the volunteer gate and then disappearing behind a row of bushes. Before they disappeared, I could see a backpack bouncing on their back.

"And that's the only time they show up on camera," Benji said, clicking on the different marks across the timeline, at one point picking the two of us up as we kissed and fondled our way back to the guest bedroom.

"Let's, uh, take off the timestamp mark for this one." Benji pressed a button, and the red tab disappeared.

"So they somehow dodged all the cameras after that first one?"

Benji nodded, his shoulders dipping. "They knew where to go. There's only a very small route between the parking and the lake that isn't covered by cameras."

He sighed, and I could tell his frustration was starting to bubble up. I let go of the chair, grabbing his shoulder instead. I massaged him, the tension inside his shoulders and neck almost instantly disappearing.

"This is a good thing, Benj."

"Really? How? We only got a two-second glimpse of whoever did it, and they were completely covered."

"Yeah, but think about it. How else could they have dodged all the cameras without knowing about them first?"

Benji rolled his head. The bones in his neck popped, and he gave a relieved exhale.

"So you're saying—"

"This isn't a crazy stranger or a stalker. I think this is someone who knows the sanctuary. Whoever hurt Tammy, whoever this Dove is, you already know them."

Benji's head dropped, and the tension filled his muscles like a stiffening poison, returning even though my fingers still kneaded into him.

No amount of deep-tissue or pressure-point work would make Benji feel better in that moment.

Instead, I just stood by him, a hand on the nape of his neck, thumb tracing soft circles on his skin as we replayed that short clip over and over again, trying to spot any discerning details in the coat-wearing figure.

11

BENJAMIN GOLD

THE COLD EVENING air felt good, even if the tips of my ears felt replaced with tiny ice cubes. The lake glittered in front of us with light from the setting sun, turning it into an orange mirror, the water like a portal into some other world. I absentmindedly scratched the top of Tammy's head while Rex worked on her back. It had been four days since the threat, and Tammy was already back to her normal and back-scratching-addicted self. Her fur still had the shape of the dove shaved into her, a nasty reminder that there was still a lunatic out there and they had it out for my family.

Sleep had been *very* hard to find these past few days, not that it was any easier to find before.

I yawned and stretched my legs across the blue blanket. It had been Rex's idea to come have some tea by the lake. He sipped from his cup, his legs crossed underneath him. He had taken off his shoes, setting them on the grass, looking like a giant's pair of shoes next to my smaller Adidas.

"Dinner was great," I said, watching as two sparrows swirled around each other. "Those ribs fell right off the bone."

"Barbecue's my thing. I don't know how to cook much else, but at least I know my way around some meat." That dripped in innuendo. Rex shot me a smirk. "I could've taken out that entire plate of ribs by myself." He patted his stomach and smiled. "Not sure if you could tell."

I wanted to reach over and rub that belly of his but resisted the powerful urge. Back when we were kids, Rex would never purposefully point out his weight. It had been a sore spot since I had met him, which had always upset me. I always thought Rex looked great, even when I wasn't sure of why I thought that, not fully understanding that men like Rex were exactly the type of men that got my blood running. He was big and smiley and hairy and so fucking hot. We hadn't hooked up since that last time in the guesthouse, but *damn* did I have a hard time thinking about anything that wasn't Rex's beautiful bear of a body standing over me, his eyes rolling back—

"Benji?"

"Yeah, what, huh?"

"I was asking if you remembered that one Christmas barbecue I had. I invited your family over. That was before my dad went full brain-washed mode. Before Sylvia really sank her claws in."

I nodded, remembering that Christmas clearly. It had been the year before our Costa Rica trip. We'd all gone over to Rex's house, and he cooked us a mouthwatering meal. They lived on a huge estate that sat right on the water, which I remembered had surprised me. I knew Rex's family had money, but he never carried himself with the kind of attitude I expected from someone who had been raised in a waterside castle. His dad was part of a fast-food chain empire, using the money to invest and grow their name even larger. He got into politics right before I met Rex.

"You cooked us these blue-cheese-stuffed burgers that I still dream about to this day." My mouth, in a Pavlovian response, started to water.

Rex laughed, nodding. Tammy rolled over so that the back scratches could become belly scratches. Her small paws, almost humanlike in their ability to grab things, scratched the air in pleasure as Rex and I doubled up on her.

"I'll have to make that next, then."

"Yes, please." Warm memories filled me. "It was a great Christmas. One of the best."

"It really was. Even if Sylvia was there, fucking everything up." Rex shook his head, eyes turning downward. "My dad always seemed uncomfortable around gay people, but he never truly seemed to hate them, not until Sylvia wrapped him up in her organization. He changed."

"I remember her treating my moms' pretty bad during that Christmas dinner."

So bad that we didn't go back the next year, and weren't invited ever again after that.

"My dad fought with her that night, I'll give him that. I was going to sleep and heard him arguing with her, saying she should have been kinder and more welcoming. That Mia and Ashley are good friends. I couldn't hear her part, she spoke too low, but it seemed to go on for a while. I just left them."

My turn to shake my head. "What a monster."

As Rex's gaze turned out toward the calm lake, I took that as an opening to admire the man sitting next to me. One I was sure I'd never connect with again, not like this. He was my brother's best friend, not mine. I didn't expect to be looking at his face again, loving the way his beard grew in, perfectly trimmed to highlight the warmth of his face, the breathtaking glitter in those cerulean blue eyes. His nose was perfect, and his ears, and the three freckles he had spread around his fore-head. His lips looked like pillows and his neck—

"You're out of it today, huh?"

Damn it, again?

I flitted my gaze to the center of the lake, hoping Rex didn't notice how blatant my staring was.

"Just thinking about a lot," I said. "What were you saying?"

"Nothing, forget it."

"No, say it again. I'm listening this time."

"I was asking if Christmas was still your favorite holiday?"

I huffed a breath. "Does a reindeer shit in the woods?"

"I don't know, does it?"

"Yes, I think."

"The North Pole doesn't have woods, though."

"Yeah, but they're flying around all over the place. I'm sure they cross woods eventually."

"So they have to wait until they're over some woods to go to the bathroom?"

I laughed, waving my hands in the air as if cleaning the board. "Yes, Christmas is still my favorite. Why?"

"Just wondering," Rex said. His tone took on a curious note. "You haven't changed much. That makes me happy. Too much shit in my life's been changing lately. It's good to know the good things sometimes stay the same."

"I've changed a bit," I said, lifting an arm and playfully flexing my bicep.

"Oh, I'm not disputing that." He smiled his toothy, bright grin.

"But you're right." I leaned back on the blanket, both hands behind me, eyes straight ahead. The sky had turned a dark purple, the stars ready in the wings, waiting to take center stage. "I don't feel all that different from the kid I used to be. You might think it's good, but I don't know, part of me is ready to change. Grow up. Get out of my moms' house and spread my wings. I thought that'd be what'd happen after college, but no one warns you that real life is nothing like the fake college life, where everything is still so contained and on track. I graduated and I'm still lost, still the same fourteen-year-old kid you met in the movie theatre."

"You're not lost, Benj. It takes time to figure things out, and I know you will. I'm three years older than you, and I feel ten steps behind you. A dropout with an impending sex tape, disappointing zealous fathers, and manipulative stepmothers all around the world."

I arced a brow. "Don't be so dramatic."

"It's the truth, ain't it?"

I couldn't argue. Most of that really was the truth, and I hated it.

It wasn't the sex tape I hated, or the dropout part either. I just hated that Rex was the one going through all this. He was a good guy with a huge heart. I spent years telling myself his heart resembled a dried-up piece of corn husk, but that had all been a lie; the text message had been a lie.

It took six years for me to try and convince myself that Rex was a terrible human.

It only took about six minutes for me to realize the complete opposite.

"Has there been any updates from the detective?"

Rex shook his head. "I'm supposed to be having a call with him tomorrow. At least the video hasn't hit the web, so I guess that's a good sign."

Without thinking much of it, I reached over Tammy and put my hand on Rex's. "It's going to be fine. No matter what happens."

"Hope so." His smile, half-cocked, seemed genuine, even though the circumstances clearly weighed on him. "If only I'd gotten a heads-up, then maybe I would have trimmed things up a bit. Made sure the lighting was good, the angles good."

That got me laughing. It was a good sign, how Rex could find jokes inside of the storm that raged around him.

"I doubt you've got anything to worry about. I wouldn't mind you from any angle," I said, the flirty line flying out of me before I could stop myself.

"Oh really?"

Crap, crap. I wasn't ready to back that all up.

Usually, I could flirt with the best of them. Back when I was feeling good about myself, I enjoyed the batting of compliments and innuendos back and forth. It was almost like the sports I found myself excelling in. There was a rhythm to it, and if the rhythm synced up, then a home run was all but guaranteed.

"Uhm," I said, "yeah. Really."

All right, so that was a strike.

Rex didn't seem to mind. He laughed, looking down as Tammy got up and readjusted herself between us so that she curled up into a ball, her paws holding on to her long tail.

"Fuck, Benj. Six years."

"I know... damn." The wind picked up and rustled the leaves, some of them falling to the ground and adding to the orange and red crunchy piles. "Did you ever think about reaching out?"

"I did, a fuckton of times. I was just so lost in my own bullshit. In the parties, in the lack of responsibilities. My dad bankrolled everything, and it gave me zero drive. When I dropped out of law school, that was it, game over. I went full steam ahead with being a closeted playboy. I lost myself. When Mav would come home to visit, I'd always come up with an excuse. I didn't want to see my family. I was scared of seeing you. I was so stupid, looking back now..."

I scratched the top of Tammy's head, her eyes drifting shut. She seemed so peaceful between us, completely unaware of the overpacked baggage we were currently unloading around her.

"I was so angry with that text, I didn't even think about it for a while. I even stopped talking to Mav for a couple of months. I was scared he'd bring you up. I think he eventually got an idea something happened, though, because he started to avoid the topic. He'd get asked about you sometimes, and he'd just shrug and say you were doing fine, but I noticed the looks he'd shoot my way. He knew."

"Really? I don't know about that. I think he would have said something to me. We're open about everything."

"Clearly not *everything*," I said, motioning between us. "What do you think he'd say?" I asked. Maverick was five years older than us and had been adopted as a baby, so he was in the family long before we arrived, but from the second Dusty and I became a part of the Golds, he had effortlessly taken on the older-brother role, teaching us how to ride bikes, how to throw footballs, how to build a computer. How to be respectful and kind and how to powerfully stand up for what you believe is right. He had all kinds of interests, and he chased them all with an impressive amount of success. It showed in his pocketbook, seeing as he was probably one of the most successful out of all of us.

Mav also tended to have a bit of an unpredictable streak in him.

"About us hooking up? I think he'd be fine with it. He's protective, but he's also level-headed. As long as we're happy, I think that's all that matters with him."

Rex had moved his hand at some point, leaving mine resting on his thigh. I didn't even realize I was rubbing him in slow circles; it felt like such a natural motion. I stopped, looking over at him. Our eyes locked and my breath hitched, catching somewhere between my constricting throat and hammering heart.

Hooking up... like the other night... I could still taste him... Feel him...

Fuck, I want him. So fucking bad.

Rex moved closer to me, but I was the one who pushed into the kiss, crushing my lips against his, unable to stop myself, never wanting to stop myself. Not with Rex, not again.

I leaned into him, making sure not to crush Tammy. I kissed him like I'd been lost at sea, coming home to my crying partner waiting for me at the shoreline. I kissed him and breathed him in and memorized his tantalizing taste on my tongue, the way his beard tickled my face and how his big hands came up to cup my head, encompassing my entire fucking face with how big they were.

A firework show of emotions blasted through me. It was a rush. An overwhelming, overheating, overstimulating kind of rush. My eyes were shut as we kissed, but I could feel tears welling up, ready to break the dam. It wasn't a sadness exactly—there's no way you could ever be sad with such a sexy hunk of man parting your lips with his tongue... No, it wasn't sadness that was starting to make me cry. It was a mix of pent-up and coiled-together emotions that had been stuffed down somewhere beneath the surface. Under the constant numbness that had been haunting me for so long.

I opened my eyes, breaking from the kiss, looking into Rex's steel-blue gaze. It felt like coming home, like being wrapped in a blue blanket pulled right from my favorite childhood moment. It was near unexplainable, considering I spent the last six years of my life convincing myself that Rex Madison *was not* the one who got away.

Not this time. I wasn't going to waste any more time. I felt like I was riding a high, straight up into the stratosphere, so I had to capitalize on it. I had to make a leap into the unknown. This was the first time in a very, *very* long time that I wanted to even make a leap at all.

So I asked my next question, leaping headfirst into the dark waters of wild impulses:

"Rex, this is nuts, but... fuck it. Would you be my boyfriend?"

And I was quickly torn in half by the great white shark of disappointment and instant regret.

12

REX MADISON

THE QUESTION CAUGHT me off guard. If we were standing, I probably would have been blown over.

I never did well with surprises.

"I, uhm, I, Benj, that's, uhm...."

I stuttered, looking for an answer. The simple one would have been *Fuck yeah. Let's be boyfriends. Let's make up for lost time and give this undeniable connection between us a real shot.*

Instead, I stuttered. And that might as well have been the equivalent of spitting in Benji's face. I watched him shut down in real time, his head dropping, his eyes shutting, back caving in.

"It's not that I don't want to be with you," I said, trying to control as much of the damage as possible as I watched our rekindling relationship drive itself off a steep ravine. "I just... it's—" *Fuck, just say yes. That's all.*

Except, how could I say yes when I was still dealing with the fallout of being deep in the closet? How could I say yes, knowing that there was a sex tape ready to drop at any second? He'd be dragged into the discourse; one way or another, he'd be affected by it.

And it would have been my fault.

Benji was already dealing with enough as it is. Could I risk adding any more on his plate?

"There's still a lot I'm dealing with, Benji. I don't think it would be fair to you. Not right now."

He nodded slowly, and his eyes turned away from mine. I stepped in it, for fucking sure. I fucked up.

"Listen, it's got nothing to do with you," I said, still trying to save something from the burning wreckage.

"No, I get it." He looked up to the darkening sky, the moon shining full and bright even though a few dying rays of sunlight still clung to the horizon. "I get it. I got carried away by it all. I should have kept my mouth shut. It was stupid."

"It wasn't stupid, Benj."

"It was. I made a mistake. It's the only thing I can really even do—make mistakes." He stood. I could see this wasn't going anywhere good, so I reached for his hand, grabbing his wrist. He looked down at me before sitting back on the blanket. Tammy must have sensed something was up. She stood, stretched with a small yawn, and went off to lie underneath a tree.

"Don't say that about yourself, Benji. You're a Gold. You're meant to do big things in your life, I got zero doubt about that."

"Meanwhile, I'm blurting out crazy questions and ruining my shot at actually being happy." He started to stand again. This time, he pulled his hand from my grip. I could tell he was beginning to spiral. His face seemed to be cast in shadow even though I could still make out every little line, every tiny twitch. "I'm not mad at you," he said. "I'm more mad at myself... Just forget it, Rex. Forget all of it. This was all a big mistake."

It hurt to hear, even though I understood he wasn't really speaking from his heart.

At least I hoped he wasn't...

I stood so that I could be at his level. This wasn't how things were going to end. I refused to believe that. I didn't even answer his question, and although it felt a little too late for me to say "yes," I could at least reassure him that it wasn't a "no." It would *never* be a "no," not for Benji.

"The only mistake is me not reaching out to you these last six years. That's the shit I regret." I reached for him again, wanting the comfort of having his hands in mind.

He put his hands in his pockets instead.

"Just give me some time," I said, trying not to throw in the white flag. "I just need a little bit of time."

"As if six years wasn't 'a little bit'?" Benji was angry. I saw it sparking in the whites of his eyes. He turned away from me, lifting his hand to wipe something from his cheek. He let out a defeated sigh and started to walk away, leaves crunching under his footsteps.

"Forget it, Rex. Forget it all."

I considered following him, chasing him even. I wanted to run after him. I wanted to say "forget everything I just said, yes let's be boyfriends, let's just fucking be boyfriends, please." The pain of seeing him walk away, head dropped in hurt, made me feel like I was splitting apart, made worse knowing that I had caused it. This threw me right back to our flight landing in the Atlanta airport, when Benji had blown up on me after that damn fucking text.

Something else in my life that I need to figure out before I can move on.

Who sent that text? And why? It ruined something that could have been incredible, and I was still dealing with the fallout. Watching the fallout storm off, resentment and anger roiling in his wake.

My hands squeezed into fists. This was not how I pictured tonight going. Not that I had any solid vision for it, but I *definitely* didn't think this would be how it ended. I thought we'd spend another night in the guest-house, hopefully a night that Benji decided to spend in my arms. I pictured us rolling around in the sheets until the sun came up. I had gotten a small taste of Benji, and now I wanted it all.

Yet I couldn't even say yes.

"Fuck." I balled my hands into fists. Tammy stirred from her spot under the tree, lifting her head, those huge honey-brown eyes blinking in my direction. Like any other domesticated animal, she seemed to have a sense when her humans were upset. She got up and hopped over to my side, where she sat on her hind legs and bumped her head into my calf, just like the cats my mom used to have.

I crouched down, scratching her head and wondering if I had made a huge fucking mistake.

"Oh, Tammy, what am I going to do."

She chirped her answer.

"Yeah, that makes sense."

My heart felt heavy. I looked toward the house, wondering if there was a boombox I could borrow real quick. This was a "rock on your window and a boombox on my shoulder" kind of moment. I hoped I didn't fuck shit up too bad, although that seemed to be my MO lately...

I started to pace around in a loose circle, looking

down at the leaf-covered ground. There was so much to think about, I could hardly even focus on one problem. They all blurred together, my blood pressure shooting up and my lungs tightening.

Fuck, fuck, fuck!

I walked to the edge of the lake. The sky, dark now, made the water seem like a black curtain had been drawn across it. Beyond the lake, I could see the thin shadow of the tall barbed-wire fence Mia and Ashley had installed after the attack on Tammy. It was a shitty reminder that someone out there wanted to hurt the Gold family.

Meanwhile, I'm doing damage just by being here.

Maybe I should have left. Should have gone to Florida. Should have never lost myself in New York. I should, I should, I should...

This was getting to be too much. This night felt like it was quickly spiraling out of control. I pulled out my phone and did the only thing I could think of doing: I dialed my best friend.

It rang and it rang. *Please, pick up, Mav.* More ringing.

Right as I was saying "fuck it" and about to close the call, I heard Mav's voice come on the line. "Rex! My dude, what's up, man?"

"Things are fucked, Mav. That's what's up." I

leaned against a tree and rubbed a hand over my face. "Fucked."

"Is everything okay there? There hasn't been another attack, has there?"

"No, no, that's all good. And Tammy's doing great, too. Your moms upped the security, there's two twenty-four-seven guards now, plus a new fence. I don't think anyone's sneaking in here again."

"Okay, good." I could hear music in the background. Another party. Mav worked hard, but he definitely enjoyed partying harder.

"You know what, I'll just call tomorrow," I said. I already felt like I'd burdened one Gold brother; I didn't need to bother the other.

"It's fine, I'm just over at Kiki's for a pregame. What's going on? You sound really beat up."

"I'm just not doing too hot right now."

"Rex, you've got this. You're going to come out of all this bullshit that much stronger. I've already got that detective working on the case, and he sounds like he's making some progress. He should have some news for us tomorrow."

"Is this the detective you've been seeing?"

"What? No, absolutely not." I could hear Mav's cocky grin in his tone. "I can't see him when he's plowing me from the back."

I huffed a nonsurprised laugh. "Well, don't distract him too much. I need him working this case."

"He's going to find whoever has that tape, Rex, and he's going to nuke it from whatever hard drive that fucker is storing it on."

I let my head fall back on the tree, the hard bark scratching me. "I really fucking hope so. I can't pick up my life and start things up again when I feel like it can all end from one stupid fucking video."

"Don't think like that. Even if the tape gets out, it won't end anything. People might talk for a few days, but that's it. And whatever happens with your dad's Senate run happens. You shouldn't obsess over shit you can't control, Rex."

"I know, I know."

"How's everything else? Has Benji been all right? He didn't sound like himself the last few times I've called."

Benji, oh Benji.

I wasn't about to update Maverick on everything that had just gone down. It didn't feel like the right time to say I was catching a major case of second-chance feelings for his little brother.

"He's doing okay," I said, looking toward the house. Benji's room had the curtains drawn without any light coming through the window.

"Keep an eye on him. I think that once Dusty's life started falling into place, Benji felt left behind. He's been so down on himself. Mia and Ash are talking about having a family meeting if things don't start getting better soon."

This was making me feel a thousand times worse about how everything went down. Benji was clearly going through it, and I just made things worse by making him think I didn't want him, when the truth was the complete opposite. "We've been getting close. I'll have a heart-to-heart with him tomorrow. See if I can help somehow."

"You two were always great at making each other smile, so do what you do best: Make my little brother happy again."

"I'll try my hardest."

A short pause and a chuckle on the other line told me Mav was biting back a joke.

"Don't be gross," I said, smiling despite myself. I joked all the time with Mav about shit like that, but the jokes never included his brother.

"I'm just saying, you've got my permission to make him smile *however* you can."

"All right, I think this call's over." I hissed into the phone. "Driving through—tunnel—can't hear."

"Can you hear this: you and my brother should fu—"

I hung up the call before he could finish. I didn't

know whether Maverick was drunk and talking shit or if he'd really picked up on the connection between Benji and me. It did make me feel better knowing that he was at least comfortable enough with the idea to joke about it, although he probably had no idea how far we'd already gone.

13

BENJAMIN GOLD

ELECTRA NEIGHED as I walked over to her with a brush and carrot in hand. She crunched into the carrot as I got to work brushing through the silky black hair. Penelope followed me into the pasture and lounged nearby. She chewed on a bone she bought with her.

It was a quiet afternoon. I spent the afternoon running laps around the sanctuary. I hadn't properly exercised in weeks, so it felt good to get the blood flowing again.

My moms had gone with Rex to go get groceries, leaving me and a few volunteers at the sanctuary. Two of them hung out in the pasture next to this one, with the three rescue horses that wouldn't fly into a murderous rage at the sight of a stranger. I could hear them chatting about school, the two college kids laughing and teasing each other about an upcoming party for their sorority.

Must have been real nice to have something to look forward to.

I set the brush down and rubbed Electra's snout. Her huge, intelligent eyes appeared to peer straight into my soul.

"We're going to be okay, right, Electra?" I rested my forehead on her. She whinnied in an apparent response.

"And we won't make fools of ourselves anymore, right, Electra?"

She didn't whinny this time. Maybe she knew something I didn't.

"No more blurting out any more boyfriend proclamations, right, Electra?"

She neighed loudly this time. I smiled and pet her forehead, her ears twitching.

I still couldn't believe myself. It had been three days since I stuck both feet in my mouth. I thought ignoring the entire situation would be the best way to handle it, except there was no ignoring Rex Madison, not when he was living in my backyard. He had tried talking to me a few different times, but I managed to run off with minimal words spoken between us.

I just couldn't look him in the eyes. I felt embarrassed and pissed and disappointed. Weird, considering I hadn't been feeling much of anything lately.

I collected the brush and bucket and gave Electra a goodbye back rub. She tossed her head up and gave a loud rumble from her lips. Penelope grabbed her bone and followed me out of the pen. She ran ahead of me as I walked back to the house. I waved at Curtis, one of the security guards my parents had hired to keep watch. He gave me a warm smile back.

"How's it going today?" he asked from inside his golf cart.

"It's going," I said. *Going nowhere.*

Curtis didn't ask anything else. He gave me a smile and got back to his patrolling.

At least I didn't ask him to be my boyfriend.

With a sigh, I started back toward the house. I didn't make it another three steps before my phone started to ring. I assumed it was my mom calling to see if I wanted anything for lunch.

"I just had a sandwich," I answered without even looking at the caller ID.

"Oooh, what kind?" That wasn't my mom's voice. It was my brother Dusty.

"Sorry, I thought you were Mom calling."

"I still want to know."

"Ham and cheese."

"Wow," Dusty said. "That's a real kindergarten

gourmet dish you've got going on there."

I chuckled. Truth was that I hadn't even eaten lunch. I hadn't been eating much at all lately, actually. I still had all the muscle I'd worked hard for over these last few years, but if I kept this up, I'd be back to my high school weight in a couple of months.

Just something else to worry about.

"How've you been, Benj? Everything good?"

"As good as it can be, I guess." I didn't want to talk about myself, though. This was my twin. He'd figure out something was up, and I just didn't want to deal with it right now. I switched topics real quick. "And you? How's the job going?"

"As good as it can be going," my brother said, throwing my phrase right back at me. He'd been working at NASA for a few years now and already had two promotions under his belt. I couldn't have been prouder of him.

"I'm on break right now actually," he said. "But I didn't call to chat about sandwiches or my job, Benj."

"Okay..." My eyes narrowed. "Why did you call? Just to say hi to your favorite twin brother?"

"That, and I wanted to make sure my favorite twin brother was doing okay... I still remember that talk we had by the lake, Benj, and I've been thinking about it a lot. How you said that you felt like something was broken... Do you still feel that way?"

I could have lied. It might have been the easier choice to make, even if it wasn't exactly the morally correct one.

"I do," I answered. There was no lying to my brother. He'd see right through the smoke and mirrors. "It's only gotten worse, Dust."

Shit. There it was. Putting words to what I'd been feeling—or rather, lack of what I'd been feeling. This felt like a "no turning back now" point. The avalanche had begun, and it roared down the mountainside, ready to entomb me in an icy white calm.

"Talk to me," he said, coaxing the words from me like a snake charmer. "Tell me what you're feeling."

"I'm not, Dusty. That's the problem. I can't feel *anything*. All the days just blur together, and I don't really know when it's going to get any better. I can't look forward to anything, and I can't look back on anything either. It's all just... blank. I really do feel broken, Dusty. So fucking broken."

"You aren't broken, that's a fact. This is something you can overcome. I shared a womb with you, I grew up watching you place first in every single competition you ever played in. You helped me learn how to read when I was having trouble, and you were speed-reading the freaking dictionary. You helped me when I wasn't saying a word to anyone, and you helped me overcome that dark period in my life. I *know* you can overcome this."

I shook my head and looked up at the cloudless blue sky. "I don't know, I'm not seeing a way out of this."

"Do you think you're depressed?" my brother asked, point-blank.

It took me a little by surprise. Such a simple, basic question. One I had already known the answer to for months, maybe even years. Still, I never vocalized it. Not even to myself.

I gave a silent nod before realizing he couldn't see. "Yes," I said, simultaneously feeling a pressure lifting from my chest and another settling on my shoulders.

"And that's okay," Dusty quickly replied. "It's okay to be depressed, but it's also important to not let it control you. Don't let the depression become you."

From somewhere inside the house, Penelope started to bark. My moms must have gotten home.

"I'm trying," I said, the defeat clear in my voice. "I just don't know what to do."

"Take it tiny step by tiny step. Focus on starting a routine again. Set an alarm, wake up early, and stick to a plan. Have you been working out? Playing any sports?"

"No, not at all. I started to run again, but I'm not sure how long it'll last."

"That's still a good step in the right direction. I think the next step would be reaching out to a professional. Have you talked to any doctors?"

I shook my head, the fear instantly spiking inside me. "I hate doctors, Dust."

"I know you do, but this is important. If someone has a tumor, they don't just put it off because they hate doctors. They go in and get it checked. It works the same for our brains."

"Says the walking brain."

Dusty tsked. "I'm serious. I want you to at least talk to a therapist. You don't have to go see a doctor, but you should at least go to therapy."

"I don't know," I replied.

"Please, Benji."

"All right, fine," I said. "I'll think about it."

I could tell my brother wanted a solid "yes," but I just couldn't give it to him. I wasn't in the mental state to even think about opening up to a stranger, no matter if they were paid and had some fancy degrees hanging up on their walls. I didn't see it helping. All I saw was the blank, empty expanse of the depression, drifting around my head like a low-hanging cloud bank.

The sliding glass door opened and Penelope ran out, chasing a red ball. Milo, the Aussie, ran behind her, wagging his tail, which being targeted by a lively Tammy.

The trio ran past me, kicking up a trail of dust. Then, through the glass doors, out walked Rex, holding a brown paper bag that looked like it was a napkin away from bursting.

"Dust, I'll call you back," I said, hoping I could dodge this upcoming encounter and lock myself in my room.

"Call me if anything, all right, Benj? And please, *please* consider what we talked about. I think it would really help."

"I will."

"Love you."

I smiled, feeling better after having talked with my brother. Maybe that was all I needed. Maybe this depression would be lifted after a few more chats with my twin. "Love you, too, Dust. Tell Brandon I say 'sup."

"I'll tell him you said 'hey, girl, heyyyy.'"

With a chuckle, I pocketed my phone and tried to keep the smile on as Rex got closer.

"Benj, there you are." Rex lifted his hand to wave. The bag he had around his wrist rose into the air, loudly tearing in half, sending a variety of different vegetables falling to the ground.

"Ah, fuck," Rex said, his expression falling as fast as the vegetables.

14

REX MADISON

SIX YEARS AGO

"AH, FUCK," I said, watching the shiny red apple fall into the grass. A capuchin monkey—Sammy was her name—came running from the tree she had been watching me in. She grabbed the apple in her hands and took a crunchy bite, looking at me as she rolled it around, taking another bite of it before turning and running back into the tree.

"She stole my wallet earlier," Benji said, coming up behind me and surprising me.

"Did you get it back?"

"No, and I've got a thousand-dollar order of bananas I have to cancel now."

That made me forget all about the stolen apple. We laughed as we took a seat on the bench, underneath a tree that had four capuchin monkeys swinging from the branches.

We'd been at the primate sanctuary for about a week now, and the trip was already coming to an end. I hated that. I wanted to stay here forever, with the Gold family, living off the land and helping animals and not having to worry about my overbearing father and monstrously homophobic stepmother.

Plus, I'd get to spend more time with Benji. That was always a huge plus. We'd gotten real close over this last week. I'd barely even hung out with Mav, and that was totally fine with me. There was something about being around Benji that made me feel better than I'd ever felt before.

"What happened to you this morning?" he asked. "I thought you were super excited to go zip-lining?"

I had been. "The heights thing got to me." That wasn't exactly the truth, but I didn't really want to talk about it.

"You said you loved heights, though?"

Crap, I did say that. "Heights from like a plane, not a rope tied between two massive trees."

Benji's brow arched. He was wearing an olive-green shirt that made his tan pop and his eyes seem to glow.

"I, um." *Fine, I'll just say it.* "I was also nervous about the weight limit."

There, the real reason why I hadn't joined the Gold family on their adventure that morning. It initially sounded like a blast, and I had been looking forward to it all week. Until I realized that I was pushing close to the 250 lb weight limit. I wasn't at that weight yet, but I was close enough to feel nervous. Not so much that the ropes would snap and send me plummeting to the jungle floor; it was more so the embarrassment I'd suffer having to be turned away. It legit was one of my biggest fears, heights being nowhere on the list.

"Seriously? You would have been totally fine, Rex. And if they did end up saying anything, I would have turned around with you, and we could figure out something else to do." His smile felt warm and genuine. "We can go again tomorrow if you're down? Just you and me. You'd love it, I swear. It was incredible."

"It sounds incredible, but..." My insecurities rose up like a sun-blocking tidal wave. I looked down, my body feeling like a prison all of a sudden.

I'd always been big, even as a little boy. I was taller than everyone in my classes, and I'd started growing wider than them, too. After my mom passed five years ago... well, it was game over. I hadn't stepped on a scale since then, having turned to eating to help with the constant pain I felt thinking about her.

And then came the insults. The snide comments. The flat-out bullying. I'd grown a tough skin throughout high school, but it wasn't tough enough to stop the trauma from setting in. I still didn't even feel comfortable driving past a high school, remembering the relentless torture I'd received from the other kids.

All that trauma, all those names, all those looks, it all came bubbling up to the surface. Unexpected and powerful. I took a deep breath but couldn't stop myself from letting out a rogue cry. Benji sat up, his eyes widening. He put a reassuring hand on my shoulder, which only made matters worse.

"I'm sorry," I said, wiping my cheeks and feeling like an idiot.

"For what?" Benji leaned in a little, his eyes meeting mine. "You've got *nothing* to apologize for. You're perfect the way you are, Rex, and I'm not just saying that. I really do think it. So what if you've got a little extra around your waist? People love that." His smile grew. "*I* love that."

A self-deprecating laugh fell from my lips. Benji wasn't one to say things he didn't mean, but still, I couldn't take him seriously. Benji was a trophy-winning sports star with a body that clearly saw the inside of a gym multiple times a day. Even here, on vacation, I'd see Benji working out, doing crunches by the beach, playing basketball with the kids from around the sanctuary, even lifting huge bags of animal food as a substitute for weights.

Meanwhile, I felt like an overweight slob. "There's

no way anyone can love this." I placed two hands on my stomach and shook.

"I'm telling you right now that I do. And I'm a thousand percent sure I'm not the only one." He looked me straight in the eyes. "And it doesn't even matter what I say, or what anyone else says. The only person who needs to love you is you." He put a hand on my chest. It felt different and right and perfect and so, so fucking needed.

"You've got to love yourself, Rex."

"Coming from Mr. Olympian here, that means a lot."

"I'm far from an Olympian." He took his hand back, leaving a warmth on my chest.

"Thank you, Benji. Even though you're like four years younger than me, I still look up to you, no matter what Mav says. I was feeling like shit this morning, and I didn't think I'd be feeling better anytime soon. I was wrong. I should have known, too. As long as you're around, it's pretty much impossible for me to feel like shit."

Benji dropped his head, as if he were bashful. Of what? And were his cheeks turning pink?

Fuck. He doesn't even know how I feel about him...

"Benji, there's something else we have to talk about."

I had to do it. This couldn't wait any longer. I knew

I was bisexual, and I knew I had growing feelings for Benjamin Gold, and I knew I had to say it all out loud. My dad and stepmom were hundreds of miles away. Benji was telling me to love myself, but I had been keeping a huge part of myself stuffed down, making it impossible to even start the process of loving who I was.

This was the start of that process.

"I'm all ears," he said, shifting on the bench so he faced me. Behind us was the home we were staying at, the sounds of laughter coming from one of the open windows.

"First, I wanted to say thank you, for being a good friend. Mav is my best friend, but you might be my favorite Gold brother, for sure."

He laughed at that, his cheeks a brighter shade of red.

"Don't tell him I said that."

"I won't."

Deep breath. This was it.

"You and I, we click really well. I don't think I'm the only one who's noticed—"

"You're not."

"And it's gotten me thinking, a lot. About, well, about—"

"Rex! Benj! What are you two doing over here? We're about to head down to the beach. Come on."

It was Maverick, walking over in his white board shorts and a beach towel thrown over his shoulder.

I'd never been more disappointed at seeing my best friend. Benji shot me a look and then, under his breath, said, "We'll talk later?"

"Sounds good," I answered, unsure if I'd even have the courage to bring it up again.

From somewhere up in the trees, Sammy the capuchin monkey finished up her apple and let it drop, the core falling off my head and bouncing to the ground.

15

BENJAMIN GOLD

I HURRIED to help pick up the fallen vegetables. Our heads almost bumped together in that dumb rom-com way that would have made me roll my eyes while wishing it was our lips bumping together.

Jeez. Five seconds in my space and I'm already back to fantasizing about him.

"Thanks, Benj." Rex said, holding an armful of veggies. He looked real good today, with his beard trimmed up and his hair swooping to the side, his bright blue eyes catching the sun like they were tiny gemstones. They matched with the sky blue of his shirt and the light blue of his jeans.

It also didn't hurt that blue happened to be my favorite color.

"These for the horses?" I asked, nodding toward the stables.

"Mostly. Some of it is going to the nursery."

"Gotcha," I said.

"How've you been, stranger?" Rex said as I started walking back toward the stables. "I feel like I haven't seen you in years."

"So dramatic." I rolled my eyes and smiled. "It's only been sixty-five years and three days." I feigned my back giving out. If Rex was going to tease me, I might as well play along. I'd already made a big enough fool of myself around him; a little more foolishness wouldn't hurt anyone.

"You look great for being sixty-something. What's your skincare routine?"

"Lots of tears and pizza grease."

"Sounds right up my alley."

"Oh, and a dash of cumin."

"Excuse me?"

"Cumin. The spice." I shot him a smirk. "Along with some come."

Rex snorted at that. I laughed along with him, feeling a spark of normalcy run through me again. This felt like the old days, when Rex and I would bust our stomachs laughing over the stupidest shit.

It was nice. Really nice.

We joked around some more, the tension I expected to feel around him completely nonexistent. I realized I had been avoiding Rex for no good reason. So what if I'd asked him to be my boyfriend out of the blue? So what if I'd curled up into a ball of fatalistic embarrassment that night and the nights that followed?

It helped that the convo with my brother had lifted my spirits, or I may have been running the opposite way when I saw Rex coming out of the house.

But my talk with Dusty helped shift things in the right direction, and I could feel my mood lifting because of it. Nothing had been cured, and there was still work to do, but just saying "yes" to his question about whether or not I was depressed, that was a huge step for me. I had been scared to admit it for some reason, that yes, I could be depressed and that I needed to see someone about it because... it was just scary. There was still such a stigma over mental health, and that stigma unnecessarily stalled me from accepting the truth and possibly dealing with my depression earlier.

We were standing next to Electra's pen with a bag of carrots, talking about a recent reality show blowup, when I could see Rex's eyes light up with some kind of crazy idea.

"What?" I asked, following his gaze. He was looking at the saddles hanging up on the wall of the stable.

"Let's go for a ride."

"On horseback?"

"Was there another choice?" he asked, the half-cocked smile of his telling me exactly what he meant.

I walked over to the saddles. My plan for the day had been to lock myself up in my room and watch old episodes of *Family Guy*, but this did sound like it could be fun. I hadn't gone horseback riding in close to a year, and there was a trail that wrapped around the sanctuary which had been one of my favorite places to be on a sunny weekend.

"All right, Chocolate Chip and Canyon are great with the saddle. I'll go grab them."

"Wait, I wanted to ride Electra."

We both looked at the towering gray speckled mare, her hair glistening like a Pantene commercial targeting the equine audience. Rex walked over and put a hand on the horse's nose. If it were pretty much anyone else, Electra would have tried to bite a finger and then proceed to buck away in a cloud of dust.

"You sure? Mia's the only one who's ridden her so far. She does really like you, though."

"Yeah, I'm sure. I'm no beginner rider either. I know my way around some reins."

"Really? I didn't think they had many horses in the city."

"I would drive out every month or so and ride. It

was something I used to do with my mom as a kid, and I've kept it up since. I toyed with even buying my own horse at one point."

That surprised me. For some reason, I partly assumed I already knew all there was to know about Rex Madison. He was my brother's best friend, the son of a famous (and to most, infamous) Georgia senator, and he was my biggest crush ever, even with thinking—for six entire years—that he had actually hated me.

"Have you thought any more about who sent that text message?" I asked, walking over to the other pen where Canyon munched on some hay. She was a dark red thoroughbred rescued from a fire that had unfortunately killed her previous owners, and unlike Electra, she was a huge sweetheart.

"I've got no clue."

"Do you remember ever losing your phone during the trip? Maybe someone picked it up and read our texts."

"No, I remember having it with me all the time. *Especially* because of the texts."

There were three days left on the trip when the dam between us broke. We kissed after an evening spent alone on the beach, and then we couldn't stop after that. Except Maverick didn't even know Rex was bi back then, so we kept things under heavy lock and key.

Except for the texts.

"My dad bought me the phone before the trip. Said it was prepaid, so I wouldn't need to do anything else with it."

Rex said it as a throwaway line.

"Your dad?" That throwaway line may have had the key. "So this wasn't a phone you'd been using before?"

"Nope," Rex said, slowly but successfully saddling Electra. There were no kicks or bucks or angry neighs. In fact, Electra seemed excited, her tail swaying back and forth in an even manner, her nostrils and lips appearing relaxed, a sign of a very happy horse.

"What kind of phone was it?"

"I can't remember. It was this mint-green flip phone. Why?"

"I'm wondering if maybe, and this could be a completely wild theory, but what if your dad had the phone bugged before you left?"

Rex looked to me, and I could see the gears spinning. His thick brows inched closer together, and a few rows of wrinkles appeared on his forehead. "You know, that isn't as wild as it sounds..."

"I could be totally wrong. But if he had access and was reading what we were sending each other, then he might be extra invested in making sure we stayed apart."

"Fuck, Benji. If it was my own father who did it— I was fine with him cutting me off. I get it. I'm an adult, I should be carving my own path. But if he—if the reason you and I—" He balled his fist and shook his head, a red flush creeping up his neck. His anger was palpable.

"Talk to him. See what he says. And just remember that whatever happened is in the past, regardless of what he says."

"Still," he said, taking in a deep inhale. He rubbed the bridge of his nose. "You're right. You're right."

"Come on. Let's forget about the bullshit for now. I shouldn't have even brought it up," I said, patting Canyon's neck, before opening the gate and guiding her out. Rex followed suit, and Electra seemed as relaxed as I'd ever seen her.

"I want you bringing it up. Whatever's on your mind, I want to hear it."

That was refreshing.

"Why did the government declassify evidence of alien spaceships and yet no one seemed to have cared for more than two days?"

Rex gave me a very confused look, his eyebrows practically touching.

"You said you wanted to hear whatever's on my mind."

He laughed, which jumped over to me. Soon, the two of us were laughing about nothing as we finished getting the horses ready. Tammy, who always seemed to be attracted by the sound of laughter, hopped out from around the corner, chirping her happiness to be around us.

"Looks like we've got a plus one," I said, getting onto Canyon's saddle.

"Should we saddle up a horse for her?" Rex asked. He got Electra moving in a slow and measured trot. Canyon fell into place beside her, with Tammy bouncing along on the side.

"I think she's better off on foot."

"On paw?"

"Yes," I said, giving him a head tilt that said *really, bitch?* "On paw."

And then we laughed again, my spirit feeling so much lighter than it had when I had woken up that morning. The smiles and rib-rattling laughs came naturally, which was such a relief after years of feeling like I had to force them. Not all the time, but most of it, I felt like I was wearing a mask. No one really saw the dark clouds that filled my head, not through the fake smile I'd been able to perfect.

Today, there weren't any fake smiles or fake laughs.

It was all genuine, and it was all so, so, so freaking needed.

"God, my mom would have loved this," Rex said. We were leading the horses out of a side gate that opened onto the wooded trail, willows draping the path with branches that were stripped of their leaves. Spanish moss clung to the branches, adding another layer of magic to the backdrop. On the other side of the trees was a river lending its peaceful sound of running water to the soundtrack of birds singing and trees rustling.

"I hate how we never met."

"She would have loved you, too. After my parents divorced, she moved back to her hometown in Puerto Rico. A few years later and we lost her forever."

"What happened?"

"A brain aneurysm. The doctors said it was so bad, there wasn't any chance of her having survived it. From one day to the next, everything just changed. Crumbled. It felt so unfair, even with the doctor saying there was absolutely nothing anyone could do. It just felt so fucked-up."

"God, I'm so sorry, Rex. A death is always excruciating, but an unexpected one, I don't know, it just, it doesn't feel fair."

"I feel like things would have been so different if she were around, too. It's probably not good to think about, but I do imagine a life where I came out early because of her support. She was always there for me, no matter what. Even when she was living an ocean away from me, I knew she had my back. She would have taken me, but I didn't want to leave my friends, my school. Or my dad."

"You guys got along back then?"

"Oh yeah. Even though my parents separated, they were both the world to me. No matter what. And I felt like I was the world to them."

"But your dad—"

"Is a raging bigot, yeah, that part is what ruined us. It didn't start until he met Sylvia, then it all went downhill from there." He let out another sigh. "It was a slow change, but she changed him for sure."

"You think there's a way of getting through to the old him?"

Rex shook his head, his eyes aimed straight ahead, one hand loosely holding the reins and the other on his leg. He really did seem like a pro at this, and Electra seemed like the perfect horse for him.

Also, Rex looked really fucking hot on a horse.

"It's all right," he said. "I don't need him. He's helped me for long enough. Now it's time I find my own path."

"Maybe you can get into politics, too? Take him out of his own seat."

Rex huffed a laugh at that, clearly not believing it as much as I did. "That'll be the day rescued river otters named Tammy start to fly."

"Hear that, girly?" I said, down to the happy little otter. "You're getting wings!"

16

REX MADISON

THE DAY WAS BRIGHT, one of the brightest. There was a kind of magic in the air that I couldn't quite pinpoint, but I could sure as hell feel it down in my bones. It rustled through the red and orange leaves, swirling around us. The trail we trotted down was completely surrounded by trees. I felt transported. Like we were somewhere else, far away, on some private island with our two horses, laughing and talking without a care in the world.

Benji's smile made that magic all the brighter. Every time he laughed, every time his eyes lit up, I felt my heart soar further into the clouds. I wasn't sure exactly what happened, but there was a noticeable shift in Benji's mood.

This was the Benji I remembered. Always so quick

to laugh and make others laugh along with him. His toothy grin could easily win anyone over.

I'd missed it since getting to the sanctuary, so every laugh and smile he gave me felt like a huge breath of fresh air.

"Look, follow me," Benji said, pointing toward a thin path that was overgrown with bushes.

"Come this way." He turned Canyon down the trail, and I followed, having to duck under some low-hanging branches. The vibes turned less scenic and more sketch, the trail thinning enough that we couldn't ride next to each other. The sun was blocked out by the thickening canopy. The shadows grew thick, the path seeming to rise in elevation although I couldn't see far enough ahead to be certain.

"Is this the part of the movie where you reveal your thirst for blood?" I asked.

"Are you saying—"

"I know what you are."

He turned and gave me a serious look. "Say it. Out loud. Say it!"

I returned his deadly serious stare, seconds from cracking up. "A secret shopper."

Benji's jaw dropped, clearly not expecting that answer. He then started to laugh, filling the air with that beautiful sound of his. I joined in the chorus.

"You read the book, too?" Benji said.

I nodded. "Read all of them."

"Annnnd?"

"Team Jacob."

Benji nodded. "Makes sense, for a bear."

It was my turn to drop my jaw. With a laugh, Benji raced ahead, Canyon picking up speed and turning a corner. I followed his lead, the sounds of our laughter and our horses echoing through the woods.

With our accelerated speed, it didn't take much longer for us to arrive where Benji had been taking us.

And again, my jaw dropped.

The narrow and wild trail opened up onto a breathtaking field of colorful flowers that reached all the way up to the crystal-clear river babbling over smooth rocks and pebbles. The river ran straight over the edge of the small hill we had climbed up, creating a beautiful waterfall, the water bubbling and splashing off the large boulders at the edge of the river.

Benji was already tying Canyon to a tree. I got off Electra and did the same, looking around at the story-book clearing. "I didn't know this was so close to the sanctuary."

"Yeah, no one did until like three years ago. It's been one of my favorite spots to hang out, although I haven't come here in a while." He looked around, like someone walking into an old childhood home, the walls feeling familiar but appearing different.

"I used to sit here and just put my feet in the water. The sounds would sometimes put me to sleep. Best sleep of my life."

Benji went over to the edge of the river. He took off his sneakers, then his socks, and he stuck his toes in the water, closed his eyes, and sighed.

"Let's sit," I said, taking off my shoes and putting my feet in the water.

Benji sat next to me, his fingertips barely a grass blade length away. I could have sworn I felt his heartbeat through the ground itself. I'd never felt this in tune with someone, as if we didn't even need words to speak to each other.

Fuck... did I fuck up?

Should I have said yes to being his boyfriend?

"It's nice, huh?"

I nodded. "Nice feels like an understatement. I needed this." I rolled my head in a circle, taking in a deep breath. "I've been so damn stressed."

"From what?"

"Take your pick, Benj. My unemployment, my lack of permanent housing, my father's rejection of me." I shook my head, feeling almost dickish for complaining. "Sorry. I know I should be the last to complain. I've been living off my dad's money and blowing it on parties and rent in New York... I guess life just caught up to me."

"You were just caught up in it all, Rex. Give your self space for growth. You can reinvent yourself, turn this low point into a high one."

"I don't even know where to start."

"Take it all one building block at a time. Your job, focus on that. You said you're thinking about going back to law school—that's still on the table, right?"

I nodded.

"Great, we'll start figuring out what you need for applications tonight, and then tomorrow we'll start putting things together. Nothing major, just whatever little things we can do for now."

I looked to Benji, who had adopted a glow I hadn't witnessed from him in so long. It made me want to lean in and kiss him, drink in some of that glow.

Fuck me, why didn't I say yes?

"Or maybe there's another option," Benji said. "Maybe you can look into getting into politics? Follow your dad's footsteps and reverse any damage he might have caused."

"I've thought about that—"

"And?"

"Well, then comes the second thing that's kept me awake at night: the sex tape is still out there. The second I step into any kind of political role, it'll *for sure* come out."

Benji didn't respond immediately, instead chewing on his lip in thought. I started to feel that same fear as before, the magma-hot brand of judgment and rejection.

"See, even you don't know what to say."

He shook his head, wiggling his toes in the water. "It's not great, only because I can see people using it as a weapon to hurt you, and I hate even thinking that. It makes my fucking blood boil. You shouldn't even have to worry about something like that."

"I really wish I didn't, but—well, I do. And it's real fucking shitty."

"Have there been any updates from the detective?"

"He's having trouble reaching the two people who I was, eh, in the tape with. Which is weird. I've always been able to contact them, and they won't even answer my calls or texts."

Benji's brow arched. "Suspicious..."

"Very." I sighed and rubbed the bridge of my nose. "I trusted them. I've known them for about two years. But if they set something up then, fuck, I'd be blindsided."

"And have there been any more threats?"

"Not yet, no." There was a question that felt like an anchor around my chest, dragging me down. I didn't know if asking it would relieve the pressure or make it worse. If Benji answered in a negative kind of way, I'd be devastated.

But, on the other hand— "Benji, what would you think of me if the video leaked?"

There. The anchor slowly loosened its hold around me. I waited, holding my breath, unsure if I'd get rid of this weight permanently.

"Honestly?" Benji asked, my heart skipping a couple of beats.

"Yeah, honestly."

Benji's hand tightened around mine. "I wouldn't think twice about it, Rex. It wouldn't change a single thing I see you in. So what, you had sex? You were a human? I wouldn't give a single fuck. And that's without even having to say how disgusted I am by the invasion of your privacy and the blackmail of your private moments. It's fucked-up, and I'd never judge you *at all* for it. You're Rex Madison: horse whisperer, moms whisperer, Benji whisperer, Tammy whisperer— all right, that's a hell of a lot of whispering. But you're also a boldly optimistic, big-hearted, and sharp-witted guy that I look up to. Nothing is ever changing that." Benji's smile was reassuring, but his words were what did it. It took that anchor of oppressive weight dragging me down and cut the chains, letting it fall to the bottom of my past.

"That really means a lot to hear," I said, unable to capture all my gratitude in a simple sentence.

So instead, I settled for a kiss. Benji gave a small gasp of surprise, his lips instantly melting against mine.

"*And* you're a kiss whisperer," Benji said, a thumb on his lips, curled into a sheepish grin. There was a rosy pink blush swirling on his cheek, which only upped the temperature in my own core.

"I seriously needed to hear that. I was worried, especially about you. I didn't want you think anything different of me. I've never wanted that, even when we were kids."

"Well, I'm glad you can breathe a little easier now." He tilted his head. "Even though you just managed to steal mine."

"I'm sure you'll get me back."

"Oh, I will." His devilish smirk made my jeans feel a size too tight, especially around the crotch area. "I'm glad you feel better, though. I like seeing you smile."

"Not more than I like seeing *you* smile."

"Okay, we aren't starting this." He chuckled before saying under his breath, "I like seeing you smile more."

"You've been smiling a lot today. I've been loving it."

He cocked his head, his smile only growing. "Yeah, I've felt extra smiley today, if I'm honest... It feels good. I've been feeling really good today."

"Any reason in particular?"

"I talked to my brother, Dusty, before you came walking in like a wrecking ball with your vegetables, and I had a breakthrough. I've been feeling really out of it for months, probably even years at this point. Just empty and numb, sometimes sad, but mostly numb. And, well, talking with him and kind of thinking about it all, I've realized that I could be clinically depressed. The ride here, with you, it kind of sealed the deal for me. I felt so happy, just so free, and I realized I should be feeling this way more often. I shouldn't be a slave to the chemicals in my brain, especially if there's a way to change things for the better.

"So." He took in a deep breath, looking out at the crystal-clear water flowing over our feet. "I've decided to make an appointment to see a psychiatrist and a therapist sometime next week. I'm done being defeated before I've even tried fighting the battle."

My heart swelled with pride and happiness for Benji. "That's one of the best things I've heard in so damn long, Benj. I've sensed the shift in you since I got to the sanctuary, and I can't imagine how hard it's been, having to go through it without truly accepting it. But you're right, now you've got a chance to actually fight back, and you will. I know you will, Benji. You're a Gold with a heart of gold and a diamond smile, and neither of those things are ever getting snuffed out. I'm so damn proud of you."

He rubbed at a tear that almost made it down his cheek. "It feels good, even just saying it. How weird, huh? Saying that I have depression feels good... but only because I feel like saying it out loud is finally giving me a shot at beating it."

"And there's no way you won't," I said, his hand still in mine, our fingers locked and our spirits twining, this moment feeling heavier than any before.

"It's crazy how good I feel just saying it."

"It's because now you have a plan of attack."

"Yeah, and I'm sure the road ahead is still pretty long, but shit, I'm actually excited for once."

"And you should be." I pulled my feet from the water and turned so that I sat facing him, grabbing both his hands in mine. Benji shifted so he faced me, too. "You've got this, Benj."

"I feel like I do, finally." He offered me a shaky smile, the emotions of the moment beginning to catch up. "It's been hard, Rex. I think I was so deep in the swamp of it that I started to feel like it was a part of me. Like the void had already swallowed me whole. I couldn't see any way out, and I felt myself accepting it. I'd just wallow in the depression, so much that days turned into hazy blurs."

"That's what depression does—it make you think

it's got control of the wheel. But that is the furthest thing from the truth, and once you realize that, then you've got the chance to take back control."

"And I will."

"You definitely will."

His dimples appeared, his eyes shining with hope and light. His hands felt good in mine—they felt *right*. Like we were somehow created to walk through this life hand in hand, never meant to separate. Not for six years or six minutes. Not for anything.

"I hate how I missed six years of your life," I said, lifting our hands and splaying my fingers, playing with his. "But I'm so glad I'm here today, witnessing you reclaim the strong and hopeful and uplifting Benji I remember falling for all those years back."

"Falling for, huh?"

"Falling *hard* for."

"Oh, is that so?"

"Very much so."

Benji leaned forward, his smile wide, the glow in his eyes sparking. Nearby, two sparrows dove and twirled, singing as they flew together to a tree on the other side of the river. The horses munched away on the grass underneath them, seeming as relaxed and happy as the two of us were.

"Six years," Benji said, "that's a lot of time we've got to make up for."

"You've got any ideas on how?"

"Eh, just one or two."

Benjamin Gold, the one who almost got away, crossed the distance between us and kissed me in a way that told me one thing and one thing only:

Benji wasn't going anywhere this time around.

17

BENJAMIN GOLD

I KISSED him without any abandon. I let the dam break, allowing myself to get carried away in the rush of blissed-out emotions. This had been the best I'd felt in so fucking long, and I was more than ready to celebrate. My entire body buzzed with a sparking kind of heat, like Pop Rocks going off inside every part of me.

It wasn't long before Rex was moving back, lying down on the ground, and I had kissed my way on top of him, our lips locked and tongues swirling. He licked my teeth, under my lips, sucking my bottom lip between his teeth and giving me a love bite.

I moaned, straddling him, the kiss quickly escalating into something more. Heat rolled off the both of us. My dick went rock hard, and I could feel him in the same state, our erections rubbing against each other through what felt like a thousand layers of clothing.

Control slipped from my grasp, lust driving my decisions. I wanted to tear off every piece of fabric on our bodies and take him right here, on a bed of rocks and grass and dirt. I wanted to rip his pants off, lift his legs up, and line myself up to feel his silky soft heat wrap around me.

"We need to get back to the guesthouse," I said, breathless against his lips.

"How fast you think we can get there?"

"We've got horses. Five minutes?"

"Let's make it three."

Another kiss and another roll of our hips before we separated. We laughed, giddy as we got back on our horses. Rex was off first, riding Electra with an expert's hand, leaving me behind in their dust as Canyon and I tried to catch up. The wind whistled in my ears as Canyon ran, hooves crunching over the leaves and twigs covering the ground.

Rex kept his lead the entire time, arriving at the stable and taking off the saddle by the time I arrived with Canyon. He helped me with the saddle, helping cut the time it took to get us over to the guesthouse. I couldn't wait for us to get in, and the second the door was shut, we were on each other again, my cock rigid and straining against my jeans.

My heart felt like it would beat out of my chest.

Meanwhile, my cock felt like it would break out of my pants.

Rex kissed me with a burning passion that turned any kind of barrier between us into a pile of ash, and I kissed him back, determined to match him. Our tongues swirled and battled for dominance, trying to get the most of him, taste the most of him.

"Oh, Benj, fuck. I've wanted this for six years. Ever since that first night."

"That velvet midnight." I kissed him again, our bodies pressing together with a hungry need.

"That velvet midnight." He spoke against my lips. I could feel his erection straining between us, against mine. I pushed my hips forward, wanting to rub myself all over him.

We kissed our way to the bed, working to undress each other on the way. Rex pulled my shirt off while I almost ripped his off, immediately kissing his hairy chest. Our pants were a little tricky since we were both still *heavily* invested in getting to the bed as quickly as possible, but we managed kicking off our pants without tripping.

I fell back onto the bed. My white briefs were tenting with a dark stain spreading from all the precome. I was so wet, you could see the pink of my dick.

Rex stood at the edge of the bed, looking like the

hottest fucking bear I'd ever fucking seen. He drove me wild, with the way he stood, confident and powerful. He palmed his cock over his black boxer briefs, rubbing his chest with his other hand. His passion-drunk smile made me pulse with need, wanting those lips wrapped tight around me.

Rex got down on his knees and gave me exactly what I wanted. He pulled off my underwear and didn't waste a second, burying his nose in my pubes before kissing his way up my shaft, his lips and warm breath on my cock already making me see stars.

Then he took me in his mouth, and I saw the entire fucking universe. I didn't know what could feel better than this. Rex's greedily sucked me into his mouth, his eyes looking up into mine with a reflection of the bliss I currently felt. He looked drunk off my cock, salivating and using that to stroke me, rubbing my balls, his fingers slipping down further, pressing on the sensitive bridge of skin.

I moaned and lifted my ass from the bed, allowing him to slide his finger further down. "Oh fuck, Rex. God that feels so fucking good."

Rex took that as an invitation to probe further with his finger, teasing into my crack. I tensed for a moment, not used to having anyone play with my ass. I usually always topped and never felt comfortable enough with hookups to let it happen.

But Rex was far from a hookup, and the ecstasy that flooded into my body as Rex's finger passed over my hole quickly overtook any second thoughts or anxieties I'd have. It was like an electric shock, but one that got an engine roaring instead of going haywire. I ground my hips, rubbing myself on his hand while sinking my cock deeper down his throat.

When he came up for air, I used that as an opportunity to get us on equal ground. "Take off your underwear and get in bed."

Rex, his lips glistening, stood back up. His cock had slipped out of the front of his boxer briefs, the dim lighting in the room catching the sheen of precome on the tip.

"Mhmm," I said, unable to wait for him to take off his underwear, not when the main course was already served. I sat up and leaned in, grabbing him in one hand. He felt warm and hard and heavy. I stroked, entranced with the velvety soft skin, the head of his cock fully exposed as I stroked.

I sucked him into my mouth, swallowing the taste of him and immediately becoming drunk off it. He had a salty sweetness that consumed me, making me wild with even more heat. I reached up and rubbed his belly, up to his chest, feeling the hair under my palm, his cock reaching the back of my throat and making me want more, more, *more*.

"God you taste so fucking good," I said, breathless, licking the tip of him, my tongue coming off with a clear rope of precome. I lapped it up before going in for more, pushing my gag reflexes to the limit. He was thick, making me stretch my jaw to fit him all.

"Fuck, Benj, *fuuuck* that feels incredible."

I bobbed up and down, stroking and sucking him, jerking myself off at the same time. The chesty grunts coming from Rex turned me on even more, if that was even possible. His toes dug into the carpet, and his hands grabbed the back of my head, steering my lips, pushing me further and further down his cock, until my nose was against his underwear.

I fucking loved being filled by him. I took it all, letting him hold me down until I had to break for breath.

That's when Rex leaned down and kissed me, sloppy and passionate. He reached down and, instead of grabbing my cock, slipped his fingers back between my legs, underneath me, his finger finding my hole and rubbing as his mouth claimed me.

I moaned, the sound torn from my chest as Rex pushed up, his finger teasing me open. Instead of tensing up, I relaxed, and I started to grind myself down on Rex's hand, inviting him in further, my nerves like live wires sparking raw in the open air.

"Get on your hands and knees," Rex said, as he

took off his underwear, his heavy cock and balls fully free, crowned by a dark bush of hair. He stroked himself, legs wide, nipples hard.

"Go," he said, urging me on. I listened, flipping over and getting on all fours.

"Mhmmm, fuck. Benji, you're beautiful. Every single part of you." One hand slowly rubbed over a cheek before another joined, massaging and squeezing. He spread me open, and I felt the cool touch of air against me, making me lean forward at the new sensation.

Rex pulled me back, hands on my hips before returning to my ass. He gave one of my cheeks a slap, short and sweet, the sting of it immediately trans-forming into a dose of pure pleasure. My moan seemed to urge him on. He opened me again, and then I heard him spit, before the wet glob fell onto me and dripped down.

Again, I wanted to lean forward, not used to this at all, but I resisted that urge and instead did the opposite. I relaxed and leaned backward, feeling myself opening even more.

Rex rubbed his spit in, circling my hole. "Ready?" he asked, his fingers pressing down harder. The only answer I could give was a half-muffled groan as I dropped my head on the bed and braced myself.

Rex pushed in, his finger sliding past the tight ring

of muscle. This moan was much louder since I had lifted my head. The discomfort I had been bracing myself for never came. Only pleasure, growing with every inch that Rex pressed into me.

"Damn your ass is needy," he said. "Still a top?"

"Maybe not after tonight," I said, gasping as Rex started to rub at my inner walls. He pressed down as he slid in and out, making my balls tighten with every move. I wasn't even touching myself and already a string of precome dripped from me.

And then Rex picked up the tempo. The wet sounds of him fingering me filled the room. I could hear him jerking himself off behind me.

"That's it, Rex, oh fuck. Fuck." He slipped in a second finger, stretching me in a way that brought another hit of pure pleasure.

He pushed in deep, curled his fingers, rubbed. Stars exploded in my vision. My cock jerked in the air, my hole tightening around him, pulling him in deeper. He grunted from behind me, the sound of him sending me right over the edge.

Without any warning, I blew, my body racked with an orgasm that threatened to split me in half.

I shouted some words, not sure what, as my balls emptied and my body jerked. Behind me, somewhere that sounded like an ocean's length away, Rex said he was coming, his statement immediately followed by the warm splash of come hitting my back, all the way up to my shoulders and neck.

I collapsed, not even caring that my chest and stomach were not soaked in my come. Literally glazed from front to back, I felt like a Krispy Kreme donut.

And I fucking loved it.

At some point, a breathless Rex returned from the bathroom with a towel for me. We cleaned up a bit, the two of us chuckling, acting as if laughing gas had been coming in through the vents. I couldn't help slapping Rex's ass a couple of times as we changed the bedsheets. And once in bed, he returned the favor by pulling me close to him and squeezing my ass, kissing me again, blissed-out smiles on both our faces.

"Well, I don't think I can move from this bed for at least a week or two."

"Same," I said, laughing as I snuggled in closer to him.

My body felt like Jell-O, from head to toes. Every move I made was slow and heavy. I threw an arm around Rex's chest. We lay there in a relaxed silence, bathing in the afterglow of our passion. I kissed his shoulder, feeling the urge to show him how fucking happy I was, lying here naked with him, body to body, warmth covering me like a blanket.

"What a perfect way to end a perfect day, huh?"

Rex said, his hands behind his head, a drunken smile on that handsome face. His beard framed those sexy lips of his, making my still-swollen dick twitch between us.

I agreed with him, kissing him again. A brief thought crossed my mind: Was I being too clingy right now? I flashed back to asking Rex to be my boyfriend, and his reaction to it, and it didn't exactly make me feel great. But being here, with Rex, our sweaty bodies fitting together so perfectly, it overrode whatever anxious thoughts were threatening to take hold. There was too much joy in this moment for even my depression or anxiety to take over. Especially not after I decided to confront it head-on. Deciding that gave me power, I wielded it.

I kissed him again, and again. He flipped over, his ocean-blue eyes like portals into another world, a perfect one.

Then he kissed me, his hand on my hand, thumb tracing over the lines of my ear.

"God, Benji, I've been wanting this for so fucking long. Just lying with you, feeling you breathe against me. I missed this so fucking much. Since that one night, I was addicted, and it took me six entire years to get another hit."

"It's a good thing it didn't take a second longer. I missed it, too. A lot."

"It feels like we turned back time without turning back the clock."

He said it perfectly. I answered with another kiss, my heart filling to the brim.

I went to sleep wrapped around him that night, and for the night after, and the one after that, too.

And every single night, so long as Rex was there, every single dream was a great one.

18

REX MADISON

TODAY WAS A BIG DAY. I had dropped a nervous Benji off at the doctor's office, promising to pick him up in an hour. That didn't give me much time to get my plan together, so the second Benji stepped into the building, I sped off, tires screeching with how hard I stepped on the gas pedal.

I'd been thinking about this surprise for a bit, so I already had everything I needed back at the guest-house, hidden away in a storage shed. I just had to get back in time to set it all up before Benji was done.

I pulled into my parking spot in front of the main house. Ashley and Mia were sitting on the porch with Aunt Gabbie, who was playing fetch with her floppy-eared beagle, Muttons. They waved at me and asked if I wanted to sit with some fresh coffee.

"That sounds incredible, Mia, but I'm surprising Benji and have to run right now!"

"Ohhh, can't wait to hear all about it," she said.

It didn't occur to me that this could definitely have pushed Benji and me out in the open, and it gave me a second of pause. Had I made a mistake? Up until now, the connection between Benji and me was private. Mia and Ashley just saw me as their son's best friend who needed a helping hand, but would they be angry if that changed into their son's partner?

Not that we're even anything official.

I sighed. We weren't official because of me, and I was reminded of that every day, especially more so in recent days, when I'd wake up to a snuggled-in Benji, his naked body like a missing puzzle piece against mine. He'd been spending every night since last week in my bed, and I didn't want that to change, not for the foreseeable future.

Hell, not even for the unforseeable future for that matter.

The storage shed smelled like wet wood and mulch. I grabbed the heavy box, as tall as I was, and brought it inside first, leaving it in the living room. Then, I went for the other boxes I had ordered online, stacking three of them and carrying them inside.

With that done, I started clearing a space in the living room. I pushed the couch closer toward the TV, moved the large bird of paradise plant to the opposite end of the room, and cleared off the mantle above the fireplace. Then I got to work opening the boxes, starting on the smaller one first.

Before I could even take out its contents, my phone started to ring.

Shit, is he done early?

I hurried to the table and breathed a sigh of relief. The caller ID showed Theo, Stonewall Investigations across the screen. "Hey, Theo, what's up?"

"Hey, Rex, got a minute?"

"Sure, yeah."

I stood up, setting the knife I'd used to cut open the box down on the coffee table. This could be worth sparing a few minutes from surprise prep.

"All right, so, I've found a few things I wanted to talk to you about, but first, I want to preface this with something, because I hate to set the wrong impression. I don't have anything solid yet."

I deflated a little. I wasn't expecting him to call and say the sick fuck was caught and the tape destroyed, but I at least was expecting big progress.

"But, like I said, I did find a few things, and I think we're on the right track." I heard a shuffle of papers from the other line. "Okay, so, I was able to track down where the camera was bought, a small tech store in Brooklyn, and the store is sending me over security footage. I don't know exactly when the camera was bought, so that complicates things, but researching the model tells me that it came out six months ago, so we've got a range to work with. I'm working on narrowing that range down, as well."

"Ok, okay, that does sound like good news to me. How much footage does the tech store have?"

"They upload exactly six months' worth of footage to the cloud."

"Damn. That's lucky."

"It is, but it's still difficult. Going through six months of camera footage isn't easy. And plenty of people buy cameras, and I'm sure many of them got this specific one. What I'm looking for is anyone we recognize to be part of your inner or outer circle. I don't want to get you paranoid right now, but it does seem to me like this might be people that have already infiltrated your life."

I nodded, leaning against the wall. "I've had that thought already... I'm guessing you haven't been able to reach either Penelope or Scott yet?"

"Actually, that's the next thing I wanted to talk to you about."

I stood up, back straight, expecting some kind of news. Those two, as tight as I felt we were, had been tossed toward the top of my suspect list.

"I talked to them both. They've been out of the

country and had both their phones stolen as they were traveling through Thailand. They talked with me for over three hours, explaining their history and connection with you. I dove into their web of contacts, as well, trying to build out a map that could lead back to you. Obviously, your father is a heavyweight in politics, and that could be having a big effect on this, but, something about this is telling me it's aimed more toward you than hurting your father."

"Yeah, because the video has my naked ass front and center, not my dad's."

"You're right."

"Sorry," I said, taking in a breath. I hadn't meant to say that with so much attitude, but the stress of it all was clawing back up. I could practically feel it using my ribs as a ladder.

"It's totally fine. This is a fucked-up situation, Rex, it is."

"When did Penelope and Scott get back from their trip?"

Theo rustled a few papers and said, "A week ago. Saturday."

"Why wouldn't they have called me..."

"I talked to them yesterday. They said they were only just able to purchase phones. I've got their new numbers here if you want them."

"Yeah," I said, going over to the kitchen. I grabbed a

pen from a drawer and turned over a Chinese takeout menu. Theo read me the numbers, totally new to me. I wondered if they just didn't have my number memorized; how would they have been able to contact me?

"All right," I said, looking at the stack of boxes I still needed to pack. The golden clock above the bar cart told me I had about thirty minutes left before I needed to head out. "Are there *any* possible suspects, then?"

"Well, I'm not taking any option off the table right now."

"So Scott and Penelope—"

"I can't say for sure. Either way. But what I can say is that I'm working around the clock on this for you, Rex. And I've got about three other detectives here at Stonewall working on it, too."

"Thanks, Theo. I appreciate it." I cracked my knuckles, wringing my hands. Anxiety started to build in me, like a rising wall, brick by solid brick. If this didn't end, if I had to live my entire life with this looming shadow over me...

"One last thing," Theo said. He suddenly sounded a little apprehensive. As if he was second-guessing whether he should say anything.

"Uh-huh?"

"I received a message earlier today. From whoever is behind these threats. Whoever has the tape."

My hand balled into a fist. "So now they're threatening you, too... Fucking shit. What did it say?"

Theo read the message. "To Mr. Sherlock 'Stonewall' Homes, keep on investigating and you'll see bigger consequences than a sex tape leaking."

It was an explicit threat. The text wasn't asking for money. It wasn't asking for anything. It was a clear warning shot.

"Fuck," I said.

Theo huffed. "It's all right. I've been doing this for fifteen years, and that's actually one of the weakest threats I've ever gotten. Trust me, on the 1-to-Zodiac Killer scale of threats, this one barely registers as a blip."

That helped me calm down a bit.

But only a bit.

"It does mean a couple things, though: whoever is behind this knows I'm involved, which brings me back to thinking it's someone closer to you than you think. I don't exactly walk around with a megaphone, shouting about my cases, so that part is interesting to me."

I nodded, my worry rising back up. It was a comfort, if a very weak one, to think that whoever was doing this was far removed from my life. Some crazy online fanatic who got lost down the wrong internet rabbit hole and now wanted to lash out at my father through me. It brought me back to thinking about Scott and Penelope.

"Another thing is that, well, frankly this person isn't very smart. They sent the text through a randomized number. Except, in order to get that number, they had to use an app and create an account with their *real* number in order to create the randomized one. I'm currently in a back-and-forth with the app company, and I'm hoping I can get that info by the end of the week."

"That's huge!" All right, back to less worrying. This conversation was turning out to be a hell of a roller-coaster ride.

"It can be, yes. So let's hold on to that. All right?"

"I will, Theo. Thank you for the update, and for all the work you and your team's been doing."

"Of course, not a problem. When Mav told me about what was going on, I knew I had to jump in and help."

Mav. Hah, they're already on nickname terms.

I'd have to bring Theo up the next time Maverick and I talked.

We hung up, and I felt much more confident about where things were headed after talking to him. The last bit of information he dropped was critical: they had a phone number. If they could get a phone number, they could track the person down to whatever ball-sweat-soaked basement they were hiding in. And there was also the lead on the tech store, which sounded like a bit of a longer shot if Theo couldn't narrow down the date, but still, it was a shot. And the tape still hadn't been leaked, even though the threat's deadline expired a week and two days ago (I'd been keeping the exact count since midnight).

Maybe I was in the clear. Maybe their text to Theo was a dying gasp. Maybe someone deleted the video by accident, or the file was corrupted, or maybe they grew a heart overnight, deciding to delete it themselves.

These were all possibilities I rarely ever entertained, except for now. I allowed myself a little bit of hope.

With that hope, I went to get back to work. I still had time before Benji was done, but I'd have to be quick. I hurried into the living room and opened all the boxes, setting them down on the floor. I grabbed a bag out of the box closet to me, tearing it open with my teeth. I took out the puffy white clouds of cotton and started to place them around the room, bunching them together in clumps on the windowsill and near the fireplace.

I grabbed the next package, opening it and pulling out the folded-up white-and-black plastic. I found the blow pin and brought it to my mouth. Before I could even start on inflating it, my phone buzzed again. I checked to see if it was Benji or maybe Theo. He might have forgotten to tell me something.

It was neither of them. It came from a number I didn't recognize.

I read the message, the blow pin still in my mouth, my eyes widening and my stomach somersaulting into my throat.

The message read:

"You have three days left. Send 500k to the account specified below and the video won't leak. Don't pay and ruin yours and your family's life. Decide."

The inflatable slipped from my mouth and floated down to the ground.

19

BENJAMIN GOLD

TODAY FELT LIKE A GOOD DAY. A *really* good one.

God, it'd been a while since I had so many of them in a row. Finally, there was a bright white light at the end of this musty old tunnel, and this one didn't lead me to any kind of pearly gates. I could actually see a better life on the other end, not an afterlife.

There would still be work that needed to be done, that was clear. I was standing outside the medical center, flipping through a pamphlet the doctor had given me about the medication he had prescribed. He warned me we might have to try out a few different ones before finding the right one, and it might take a couple of weeks to even feel any effect, but if how I felt walking out of there was any indication, then things were on the right track.

Rex pulled up in my car, window down and waving like a parent picking up a kid from school.

I couldn't help but laugh. I got into the passenger seat, the drive back to the sanctuary so short that it didn't make sense to switch.

When he asked me, "So how was school today?" I started laughing even harder.

As he drove out of the lot, he put a gentle hand on my thigh. "Seriously, though, it looks like it went well?"

"Very well," I said. "Obviously, nothing is cured yet, but he did diagnose me with depression and walked me through a few different options for medication. I feel good, Rex. I really do."

"I see it in your eyes. There's a light in there."

"That could just be the RedBull I drank earlier."

Rex laughed, although it sounded a little clipped. "I'm real fucking proud of you, Benj. I really am."

"Thank you, but it's something I should have done a long time ago."

"That doesn't matter. What matters is that you did it, and because of that, you can get your life back."

I nodded, looking out at the passing trees. A pasture of spotted cows zoomed past. "You helped a lot. I kept feeling sparks of my old self around you. It was enough to remind me of what this depression was stealing from me."

"Well, honestly, I feel like this was all you, and I

can't take any credit for it. But even if there was a tiny bit of credit there, it's really the least I can do. You saved my life back when we were younger. When I felt so fucking angry with myself, with my weight. I let other people's assumptions and judgment get through to me, and it wasn't until you taught me how to accept myself that I truly did. And listen, I'm not saying I'm fully there. I am loving the idea of being a big bear, and it seems like you love it, too—" He gave me a look that had me blushing. "—but it's hard. And so, even now, you're helping me accept myself. Every day. You've been helping me, all this time."

His hand squeezed my thigh, rubbed. Rex's jaw flexed as he looked straight ahead. Was he fighting back tears?

I put my hand on his. My fingers slipped through his, and he held on tight.

"Anyways," Rex said, pulling him together with a deep breath. "I've got a surprise for you. Back at the guesthouse."

"Oh really?" I perked up. "Interesting. Very, *very* interesting... What is it?"

"Nice try," he said, chuckling. But again, his laugh cut short. His forehead wrinkled and his eyes seemed to look somewhere further off than just the empty road ahead.

"Rex, everything's okay, right?" I had to just ask.

After coming out of an hour chat with a doctor asking question after question, this one came out pretty easily.

"Yeah, yeah, everything's good." The way his tone inflected made me think *everything* might have been an exaggeration.

"You sure?" I asked, prodding a little deeper.

He rolled his neck, and I heard a few loud pops. "Yeah, I'm sure. I've just been focused on pulling this surprise off, that's all."

Steering things back to the surprise. I smiled, feeling the excitement from Rex rising, but I couldn't box away the nagging doubt that nipped at my heels. Something was up with him, although it was clear I wouldn't be figuring it out on this car ride, seeing as we were already pulling up to the security gate at the front of the sanctuary.

"Curtis!" I said, cheerily waving over Rex.

Curtis returned with an equally as cheery "Hey there, fellas!"

He pressed the button in his booth, and the heavy iron gates in front of us rolled open. I'd gotten used to this already, but it did take me a few days to accept that this was our reality now. When I was growing up, the sanctuary only had fences for the enclosures. We never had to worry about keeping people out, only about keeping animals in.

Not anymore. Not since the Dove flew into our

lives, threatening to shut us down if we didn't do it ourselves. These days, there wasn't merely a physical fence around the entire property, but a digital one, too. Alarms would trip if anyone climbed any section of the wall and we'd all be immediately alerted.

Again, I had a difficult time accepting it was our reality, but the sense of safety was very much welcome.

Rex pulled into the parking spot, next to my mom's van. I hopped out and started down the brick path that wrapped around the house, toward the backyard. Rex caught up to me, putting a hand on my lower back for a split second before taking it off.

Damn, did I wish he had left it. I wanted to walk hand in hand with him.

Was I falling too hard? Too fast?

Yeah—six years too fast.

I set aside the needless worries and instead braced myself for whatever surprise waited for me on the other side of the bold blue door. Rex put a hand on the knob, his smile making his eyes crinkle.

"All right, you ready?"

"Yes, ready."

He cracked the door open but froze. "Wait, wait," Rex said. "Cover your eyes. And don't peek."

I listened, putting my hands over my eyes and shutting them tight. Rex's hand landed on my hip as he guided me over the threshold and into the guesthouse.

"Can I open my eyes?"

"Not yet, hold on." I could hear Rex move further from me. He fiddled around with something. A cable? What was that sound... Mariah Carey started crooning from the surround sound speakers, the familiar jingle of one of my favorite songs making me suddenly giddy.

"All right, open."

I dropped my hands and then my jaw.

The guesthouse living room had been transformed into a winter wonderland, with fake snow on the floor and clouds of it on the windowsills and across the couches, all made to seem dreamlike with the green and reds and whites of the smart light bulbs, which slowly shifted between those colors. The ceiling had a trail of mistletoe, hanging in a single-file row, leading all the way to the bedroom. There was an inflatable snowman next to a group of dancing elves, their animatronic motion smooth enough to make them look real. The windows were coated in a dusting of snow, with festive phrases written on them.

None of that compared to the stunning Christmas tree sitting next to the fireplace, a tall and bushy tree with thick pine needles and a perfect arrangement of golden lights twinkling between them. The ornaments were blue, silver, and gold, all three of which happened to be my favorite colors. The star sitting on top glowed like a bright crown, casting rays of light onto the ceiling.

"I can't—this is—" I put a hand on my mouth, unsure if the next thing out of my mouth would be words or a sob. "Nicest thing anyone's ever done for me."

Okay, not a sob. My throat did get hitched on a few words, though.

"Oh, good, so you like it."

"Are you kidding me? I love this." I made a full circle, taking it all in, Mariah belting out exactly what she wanted for Christmas.

"I got nervous, Thanksgiving being two weeks away and all, but I thought you deserved a little bit of holiday joy. Who cares if Santa came early?"

"I don't care at *all*." I turned to Rex. "As long as he comes twice." A wink his way got his cheeks turning red.

Good, that's a little payback.

"Seriously, what the fuck." I put my hands behind my head, an insurmountable level of love rising inside me. "This is amazing."

I went over to Rex, who stood admiring the scene like a proud artist looking at his work in a gallery. I fell into his arms and looked up, seeing a mistletoe conveniently placed directly above us.

"You planned to stand here the entire time, didn't you?"

He smirked. "Maybe."

I kissed him—mistletoe or not, there'd be no way I wasn't getting his lips on mine. He wrapped his arms around me and held me tight, his lips pressing against mine, same as his body. His beard scratched against my stubble. The kiss was soft and slow, our lips only barely parting, but his taste still flooded through me.

I really didn't think this day could get any better. Like, at *fuckin'* all. This felt like the peak. There'd be nothing that could happen that would make this an even better day than it already was.

"Benji," Rex said, his blue eyes locked on mine, lips shining under the shifting lights. "I've got to ask you something."

And then, just like that, I was about to be proven wrong.

20

REX MADISON

THANK GOD, he loved the surprise. I worried for a second that it might have been too much. Too extra.

But he loved it, and it showed through the glow in his eyes.

Hopefully he loved what came next equally as much.

"Benji," I said, my heart rate spiking and my mouth going dry, "I've got to ask you something."

He cocked his head, still smiling, still shining. "Yessss?"

"Well." Shit. I didn't even think of how I was going to do this. I'd been so focused on pulling off the Christmas surprise, I didn't think about what came next.

Looking into Benji's eyes, his hands in mine, it made me realize that I didn't need to plan this part. I let the words flow. "Ever since that night you asked me to be your boyfriend, I've been hating myself. I shouldn't have reacted the way I did. It was a reaction that came from fear and self-doubt, all of my own bull-shit that I projected onto you. It wasn't fair, and it wasn't right." I lifted his hands in the air, pushing my fingers through his. "That's why I want to make things right. So, Benji, would you be my boyfriend?"

There, the words came to a rolling stop. My nerves rocketed through the stratosphere. I'd been on a roller coaster these past few hours. With the recent text threat still feeling like it had a tightening grip around my throat, this moment only heightened the anxiety roiling around inside me like a wild tornado. Benji's face, although still smiling, was slightly unreadable. He seemed to be in a little bit of shock.

Crap, was this a bad time? Was this all too much?

Fuck, fuck, fu—

"Yes, Rex, let's make this official."

—ck yes!

I went in for a kiss that sealed the deal. The dotted line was signed, sealed, and delivered.

"I'm done with hiding, Benji. I'm going to come out, post about our relationship, and end all the stupid rumors. I can't let my dad keep affecting me like this. If it messes up his career, then he can go reinvent himself with an Etsy store or something. I don't care. I just want to be happy, and the only way that happens is with you."

Benji's smile only widened.

"I'm so fucking happy we got a second chance at this."

"Almost feels like the third, and we all know what they say about that."

"Coming in third is for the turds?"

That got a belly laugh out of me. Benji's laughter joined mine, his hands falling to my hips.

"I do think this time is the charm," Benji said when the laughter died down. "Whatever number we're on. I feel the difference this time."

"I do, too."

More kissing, more fondling.

More *heat*.

More, more, more. I wanted it all, and I planned on getting it tonight.

I found the hem of his shirt and lifted, Benji raising his arms and snapping them back on my body the second he could. Our kiss still feverish, our bodies moving with hungry intent.

We were butt-ass naked in a matter of seconds. Both of us were rock hard, our cocks battling for space as our bodies pressed together again, lips locked and hands roaming. I felt the smooth muscles that twitched through his shoulders, down his back. I felt the soft rise of his ass, grabbing a cheek and squeezing. He moaned into my mouth, and I greedily swallowed it, my cock throbbing between us.

"God, you're so fucking hot, Rex." Benji took a step back, appreciating my naked body with his hungry eyes. It struck me a little, seeing his perfect body and hearing him say I was the hot one. His words stoked the flames. My cock oozed precome.

Benji reached for me, his fingers wrapping around my shaft. He thumbed my wet slit, bringing it to his lips before pressing it against mine.

I sucked, still tasting my precome on his skin.

Benji didn't stop there. He dropped to his knees, his hands rubbing up and down my thighs. He looked up at me, smiling as he licked me. He flicked his tongue across the head of my cock, pulling a groan up from my chest.

"Suck it, baby. I want to feel your lips around me."

He complied, opening his mouth and taking me in. His warm lips worked me, the intense heat and slick wetness of his mouth driving me crazy.

His head bobbed, up and down, hand jerking off whatever didn't fit in his mouth. The sound of his wet blowjob was louder than the Christmas song playing on the speaker, giving an entirely new meaning to holiday joy. My eyes shut and I let myself drift off into the ocean of bliss that surrounded me.

Soon, though, my body started to cry out for more. I looked down to see Benji's thick cock twitching between his legs, and I knew exactly where I wanted it.

"Benji, come up." He licked me from balls to tip before getting back on his feet wearing a cock-drunk grin.

"Mhmmmm," he said, leaning in and kissing me with his wet lips. Our hard lengths pressed together again, building up the pressure in my balls.

"I want you to fuck me," I said, biting his bottom lip.

His eyes turned into furnaces. I could practically see the steam rising off him.

"Wait here."

I turned and went into the bedroom, walking straight to the nightstand. I grabbed a condom and the small bottle of lube. Benji stood in the living room, his cock jutting out from him. It drove my hunger. My hole pulsed, my body feeling empty and crying out to be filled by him.

We locked into another kiss before Benji took the condom from me, rolling it on.

"Get down," Benji said, "on your knees." His tone took on an authority I hadn't heard before from him.

I could have come right fucking there.

Instead, I listened, getting down on the rug, my palms and knees on the soft fabric. I arched my ass out, showing him how ready I was. His hands glided over my ass, spreading me apart. I moaned and dropped my head as I felt the cold lube squirt onto me and drip down. Benji used a finger to slide it up, in. Another moan rose up as Benji slid his finger inside me.

I needed more, though. A finger, two, three, it wouldn't do it. I needed Benji's thick cock stretching me open.

"Fuck me, baby. Fuck me."

At this point, *please* was the next word out of my mouth. The burning need to feel his heat consumed me.

The head of his cock pushed against me. I instantly relaxed, knowing what came next: immense and undeniable pleasure. He spread me open with his hands, and his cock slid in, past the first ring of muscle, making me cry out in bliss.

Finally.

Benji pushed in harder, sinking in deeper. Every inch felt like hitting a new jackpot. The stretch carried a burn with it, but only slight, barely even noticeable. Nothing compared with the intense heat and sensation of fullness that rocked through me.

"Oh fuck, Rex, your ass feels so fucking good."

"It's yours, baby. Use it."

Benji took that as a green light. He sunk into me, fingers digging into my hips. He pulled out, almost leaving me empty again, before slamming back in. I cried out as he started to fuck me harder and harder, the tempo rising and the temperature going with it. Skin slapping skin drowned out whatever holiday song played through the speakers.

He rocked into me, my body quivering, my legs shaking. My balls tightened, I could feel the edge getting closer and closer with every thrust that buried Benji deeper inside me.

"That's it, oh fuck, fuck, baby." My cock slapped against my stomach with every time Benji plunged into me. He rubbed against my prostate with every thrust, sliding over it, pressing it down, and my cock leaked onto the rug beneath me.

Then he slowed down, and he pulled out completely. I was left with an insatiable need to have him back inside me.

"Flip over, onto your back."

The command still dripped from his voice. A delicious shiver rolled down my spine. I got on my back, my legs still trembling as I opened for him. He grabbed my ankles and lifted my legs higher, my wet hole ready for him. I grabbed my dick and stroked, squeezing out another clear thread of precome as Benji lined himself up.

His gaze seemed clouded over with lust. He kissed my foot, my ankle, nipping at the skin as his cock pushed back in, meeting no resistance. His lips turned into the shape of an O as he sheathed himself inside me, balls-deep. My heart beat with anticipation as Benji gave me what I wanted, picking up the speed, thrusting into me, making my entire body shake under him with every fuck.

I looked at Benji and nearly lost it. His body, slick with sweat, was unbelievably hot. His six-pack rippled with every rock of his hips, his chest dripping with sweat beads, his shoulders broad and his arms flexing as they held my legs up in the air.

I couldn't take it. I crashed into my climax, shouting out as I grabbed my cock, ropes of come shooting through the air. My hole pulsed around Benji. He continued to fuck me, pushing it out of me. His grip tightened around my legs as he dropped his head back and matched my shout with one of his own.

He came, filling the condom, twitching and spasming with every shot inside me.

When he finished, he caved inward, falling on top of me. I wrapped my arms around him and kissed him, the two of us smiling even though we were soaking wet messes.

"Fuck," Benji said, breathless, lips lazily pressed against mine.

"Fuck," I parroted. I felt sore in the best way possible.

"I think that makes up for those six years, huh?"

"I'm not so sure. I think that probably counted for about two."

"So, by that math..."

"Yup, at least two more times tonight."

He kissed me again, his hands slowly rubbing up and down my sides.

"Plus, since we're boyfriends now, that's kind of in the description," I said, as if he needed a reminder.

I know I sure as hell don't.

This felt right. Beyond right. This felt predestined. Like everything, even the speed bumps and detours, were all leading to this very moment. Maybe it was the *only* way this could have come to fruition, this connection between us. Maybe if we had explored it sooner, it would have crumbled and cracked. The six years that separated tonight from our first time together was bitter, no doubt about that, but what if we needed that time apart to truly appreciate this time we had together now?

"I think I can handle that responsibility." Benji's came between us, and he playfully cupped my balls, rolling them.

"Oh, I know you can."

We kissed again, rolling on the floor, moving to the bed at some point. Not sure when exactly. All I was sure of was that Benji and I were meant to be. Nothing could tear us apart, and nothing could ruin the intense high I rode with Benji as my boyfriend. My one.

Nothing.

Nothing at all.

Well... except maybe one thing.

That fucking tape.

21

BENJAMIN GOLD

WAKING up in my boyfriend's arms for the past couple of weeks felt like heaven. I loved it. Things started *finally* feeling right in my life. And not only because of Rex, but also because I'd gotten help for my depression. Weekly therapy sessions helped exponentially, and I was already beginning to feel the effect of the medication. Sometimes, chemicals just go haywire, and they need a little help getting back on track. No one would leave a live wire sparking in the wind; they'd call an electrician and get it fixed as fast as possible.

That's what I felt happening in my own head. Like the wires were beginning to reform, connecting in a way that allowed me to *feel* again. A lot of the common thoughts of depression hitch it together with a deep sadness, but I had found that I couldn't even experience the sadness, much less the happiness or excitement or thrills that life normally had to offer.

Not anymore. I was beginning to experience it all, although I had to admit that the one emotion taking center stage lately was *mainly* arousal. If that even classified as an emotion.

Rex stayed on my mind pretty much twenty-four seven. I'd wake up thinking about him, have lunch thinking about him, take a shower thinking about him. Most of those thoughts left me rock hard, leading me to go find him so we could handle it together. We fit together in a way that seemed otherworldly.

Today, we were spending lunch by the lake after having snuck away for a midmorning quickie. It had been difficult keeping my hands off Rex. A week into us being official and both my parents already knew. They had simply dropped nonchalant comments about me and Rex looking good together, which I appreciated. It didn't need to be a whole moment. That I figured would be reserved for Mav, who I figured would accept me and Rex together, but then again, anything could happen. I certainly didn't want my older brother flipping and upset that his best friend and I were dating. It could certainly complicate things, and I understood that, but I had a feeling Mav would put my happiness and future first.

"Look, check out that cloud." Rex pointed up past the trees. "It kind of looks like a teddy bear."

"Really?" I tilted my head and tried to find the angle Rex was looking. "It kind of looks like a dildo to me."

"Everything looks like a dildo to you, Benj."

"Touché, touché." I laughed and side-bumped him.

"I do see the dildo, though."

"I told you!"

More laughter, loud enough to scare a few birds from the nearby trees. The winter chill started to nip through the air, but it was nothing a light sweater couldn't keep at bay. Around us, the trees were all mostly different shades of fire red and setting sun orange, with a few bright yellows dashed throughout.

"I signed up for the GRE. I take it in a couple of months. Gonna help me study?"

"Fuck yeah," Rex said, enthusiastically.

"Awesome. I think I should be fine. I already ordered a ton of study guides—should be getting here Friday. Then, well, who knows."

"I know—you become a world-renowned veterinarian, saving animals left and right, eventually signing a deal to have your own TV show that turns out to be the longest-running vet show on TV."

I looked over at those crinkling deep blue eyes. "You really thought it out, huh?"

He shrugged and said, "Nah. I just believe you can do anything."

"Thanks, babe." I kissed him on the cheek, his beard tickling my lips.

Rex's phone buzzed, catching my attention. I looked down between his lap (somewhere my eyes naturally already drifted to) and saw a familiar name on the screen.

"Your dad?"

Rex let loose a sigh. "Yeah. Third text today."

I knew his dad had been trying to reach out for weeks now. I didn't realize it was that often, though.

"Here, you can read it." Rex passed me the phone.

"Rex, please," the message read, "call me back. I'm begging you, son. I need to talk to you."

I looked to Rex before looking back out at the calm waters. The lake in front of us seemed so peaceful and serene, but I could tell the exact opposite scene was going on inside Rex's head. A storm had circled his eyes, clouding his gaze.

"How often has he been reaching out to you?"

"About every day, now."

"And you haven't responded at all?"

"No." Rex shook his head. His hand moved from mine, and he rubbed his knees. "He pushed me away, when I needed him the most, and sent me off with an overflowing bank account so that I wouldn't be hanging out under his shadow. He chose his side. My step-mother held a rally upholding 'traditional marriage,' and my father went. What the fuck is that? And what the fuck is even 'traditional marriage'? Is she talking about men and women only being together, or does she want to dig further back in 'tradition'? When interra-cial marriage wasn't allowed? Or even further? How many 'traditions' is this fucking bigot going to hold on to? Meanwhile, she's married a divorced man, likely being the one who caused the divorce in the first place, and I'm sure as fuck she eats crab like every other week. Give me a fucking break. 'Tradition.' Why don't we start new traditions, how about that?"

Rex rubbed the bridge of his nose before letting out a prolonged exhale.

"Sorry. I clearly have a lot to say on the subject."

"Listen, your stepmom sounds like a raging, short-sighted, homophobic bitch who deserves to wear ill-fitting pantsuits and get terrible haircuts for the rest of her miserable life." Rex's laugh helped reassure me a bit. "But maybe there's still hope for your dad. He's the one trying to reach you, not her."

"I just don't get it. How did my dad go from my mom, a woman who had a heart big enough to care for every single person on this planet, to a woman who has the heart of a shriveled-up prune. It's so fucked-up."

"It is. It really is."

"He deposited all the money back into my account, too."

"Really?"

Rex nodded. He took a long sip of the bubbling champagne. "I don't know what he's getting at, but I don't need it. I've lived without him so far, I can keep going."

"You have and you should definitely be proud of that..."

"But?"

"But... I think something's going on, and I don't think family ever breaks, no matter how stressed the bonds are. Even families like mine, brought together over time, our bonds are stronger than diamond, and I really don't think yours are any different... I'm just saying—"

"I should talk to him."

"You should talk to him." I reached for Rex's hand. "It won't hurt. You're in a good place, and you have a plan set for the future. You said it yourself: you don't need him. But, and I don't know for sure, to me, it kind of sounds like he might need you."

Rex chewed on that for a long moment. The birds filled the silence with their lilting songs. From somewhere in the center of the lake, a fish breached the water, before splashing back in.

"I think you're right, Benj."

I know I'm right. "Like I said, I don't know. But that's what I feel in my heart."

He leaned over and planted a wet kiss on my lips. "And that's why I fell so damn hard for your heart." He stood up and started packing up the sandwich bags and plates we brought with us. I joined in helping him clean.

"Wait," I said, realizing something. "You're going now?"

"I'm going now." Rex's face was set in determination. His thick brows didn't waver, and his jaw seemed tight.

"All right," I replied, making a decision right there on the spot. "I'm going with."

"Huh?"

"Not like, inside the house with you. But it's a long drive—I'll go with you. I'll bring a book, so I can sit in the car while you talk to him."

Rex appeared about to protest, but I grabbed his hand and tugged him toward the house before he could say a word. "Come on. Let's get there before it gets dark."

I already knew where Rex's dad lived because I'd been to his house back when we were kids. Mav had brought us over for a Thanksgiving dinner, Rex's dad being the governor at the time and living in the governor's mansion, about a two-hour drive from the sanctuary. It had been an experience I really wouldn't forget anytime soon. Once he went up to the Senate, he stayed in the same neighborhood but moved to a more modest house, a place I also visited for a Thanksgiving dinner one year.

"You sure?" Rex asked.

"Yeah, I've got nothing else to do. Besides, I'll make sure you stay awake on the road."

"Yeah, I've got a feeling what you're planning on doing may just distract me as much as sleeping."

I shrugged and said, "We'll see." He slapped my ass as I walked in front of him. I jumped and chuckled. We walked through the house and only spotted my sister, who had a mess of dog food bags in front of her and a chaotic group of wagging tails at her feet. We waved at her and quickly ducked out of the kitchen, heading toward the car. I didn't want Rex to second-guess this, and with two hours ahead of us, there seemed to be plenty of time for second-guessing. The sooner we got to his dad's, the better.

We got into the car Rex was renting, a tiny thing with rattling suspension and shaky wheels. For some reason, I started feeling nervous, and all I had to do was stay in the car the entire time. I wondered what Rex was thinking...

"When's the last time you guys spoke?" I asked as Rex reversed the car.

"A couple months ago, when the first threat hit both our phones. He called me and sounded upset, but Sylvia snatched the phone and started shouting something, so I just hung up. That was the last time."

"Okay... so... not great."

"Nope."

"Still, tonight's going to be different. Just make sure Sylvia isn't in the room. Or the house. Maybe even the state—can we make that happen?"

Rex laughed, a buzzing between his legs distracting both of us. The buzzing didn't stop. It wasn't just one text; it sounded like an avalanche of text messages. Rex mumbled a "what the fuck" under his breath as he parked the car and looked down.

"No..."

"What?" I sat up in my seat. "What's going on?"

"Oh no."

Rex's face turned a sickly shade of pale. Any color in his cheeks instantly blanched. He furiously tapped at his phone screen. In a few seconds, a video filled the screen.

Then it was my turn to go pale, the blood draining out of my body in one fluid moment.

On Rex's phone screen, in full color and sound, was the secret tape that had been filmed between him and the two other people. Rex stood there, naked and in full view, climbing onto the bed.

I had to look away. This was sickening. This invasion of privacy equaled a stab with a butcher knife straight through the chest. I looked to Rex, whose eyes were glued on the screen, his head slowly shaking back and forth.

"No, no, don't watch. You don't have to watch." I tried reaching for the phone, my instincts shouting at me to do something. He snatched the phone away, staring, fixated on what was happening on the screen.

"Rex, please."

"I'm done. It's over. It's out."

"You aren't done. Don't ever think that. This is fucked-up, dark, and completely fucking unfair. Whoever taped this and leaked it deserves to rot in jail."

"I—Jesus. Everyone's going to see this, see me. And look at me. Look at how big I look."

"Rex, stop that right now." I tried turning his face so he looked in my eyes, but he kept staring down at his phone. "Rex, listen to me. You are *literally* fucking perfect. Everything about you. Your smile, your eyes, your laugh, your humor, your pride, and yes, your weight. Everything is perfect. I wouldn't change a single thing, and I don't think anyone in their right mind would disagree with me. You can't be the only one to hate yourself. It doesn't do any good. Trust me."

Please, please listen to what I'm saying.

I watched his face, tried to see if my words landed. All I could see was the reflection of the timeline he scrolled through on his phone.

"It's already trending. The video's already fucking trending." Rex continued to scroll, and I really started to get scared. My words didn't land. I could visibly see him shaking. This looked like a spiral. Like a car hydroplaning into a spike-filled ditch, no stopping it.

"Fuck. Fuck!" Rex slapped his hand against the steering wheel. Once, twice. Three slams. Four.

"Fuck!"

"Rex, calm down—Rex, listen to my voice. It's okay." I held on to his forearm, stopping him from hitting the wheel anymore.

"I thought it was done. After the tape wasn't released with the last deadline I'd gotten. I started to even forget about it for a few seconds, but fuck, that'd be the longest I hadn't thought about that tape since it fucking started. And now—fuck!"

He threw the car in drive and went forward the few feet back into the parking spot, braking hard. He snatched out the keys and got out of the car, slamming the door shut, leaving me in the weirdly silent car.

Fuck.

22

REX MADISON

MY WORLD FELL APART the second I hit Play on the video. The image was clear, the sound as well. There I was, my body center in the camera, the New York skyline behind me, appearing like a set of eyes blinking with malice. Watching me the same way thousands would be watching me right now.

I left Benji behind and went straight for the guesthouse. My vision tunneled inward. Mia said something that didn't quite register, and nothing Benji was saying behind me landed. All I could think of was *that's it. This is the day the guillotine dropped.*

I went straight for the bathroom, dropped to my knees, and threw up. As if that would purge my body of the dread and doom that pushed at the very fibers of my being.

On the bathroom floor, my phone continued to

play the video on a loop. It was short, relatively speaking, cutting off right before I noticed the camera and launched it against a wall.

I picked it up, and instead of turning it off, I watched. I sat on the bathroom floor and watched myself. Like morbidly watching a burning car wreck, my eyes glued themselves to the screen. Even though my hand shook, the image remained clear.

There I was. Naked, bare, violated.

And fuck... I looked huge. It made me somehow feel worse. I didn't think it'd be possible to feel any worse, but I managed. My stomach turned into a pit of pure despair. I couldn't take my eyes off the video, playing on a loop.

Even when my eyes filled with tears. When the screen blurred as if I was looking through dirty glasses. It didn't matter. I could still the see the shape of me, feeding the shame that gnawed at my insides. How? How would I ever move on from this?

I managed to exit the video, only to get slammed with hot takes from random strangers online, sharing the video as if they had all the right in the world to. I read a few comments but couldn't keep scrolling. None of these people knew me. They didn't know the circumstances behind this tape, and no one seemed to care. They just reveled in the drama and the take-downs. Not all the comments were bad, but that didn't matter. One hateful tweet outweighed a dozen kind ones, every single fucking time.

Nothing mattered.

The phone dropped back to the floor. I took a breath. I needed to somehow regain control. This intense spiral had to be stopped. I got up from the floor and went to the sink, letting the water run ice-cold. It pooled in my cupped hands. I splashed it across my face.

Again, and again.

The man staring back at me, face dripping wet, was the same man from the video, and yet somehow, I looked like a stranger to myself. I didn't recognize my face, my beard. My stomach.

Benji can do so much better than me.

The negative thoughts gained control. Cold tap water did nothing to hold them at bay.

He doesn't need to deal with all my bullshit.

Water dripped down my chin, wetting my shirt, darkening the gray in splotches across my chest.

He doesn't need me.

Benji could have anyone he wanted. His entire life was on the upswing; meanwhile, mine was taking a nosedive straight into the dirt. It didn't make sense for me to hold him back, even though his words still rung in my head: "Everything is perfect."

I didn't see it that way. And now my naked body

was being shared across the internet without my consent. This was far, *far* from perfect.

My phone, already barraged with text messages, started to ring. I looked down, ready to deny the call. Whoever it was, I didn't care. I didn't want to speak to anyone.

Not even Mav.

I hung up on my best friend. He must have stumbled on the leak. He called again, and I hung up again. What could he possibly tell me that would make any of this all right? It would be a waste of everyone's time. No, I just needed to sit in this bathroom until the sun went down and I could figure out what my next move would be. Maybe I could use the money before my dad took it back? He'd definitely be emptying my account now. This leak was meant to hurt him as much as it was meant to hurt me, if not more so.

More ringing. I went to hang up, but my finger slipped, accepting the FaceTime call. Maverick's worried expression filled my screen.

"Rex, Rex, don't you dare hang up. Where are you right now?"

"In the bathroom. The guesthouse."

"Okay, okay. Good. Just breathe, Rex."

I listened to his suggestion, focusing on my breath. It didn't help much. My breathing started coming in short waves, the precursor to a full-blown panic attack.

"I'm so sorry Theo couldn't find the tape before it leaked, but you have to be strong right now. This looks like a massive iceberg in front of you, but in the rearview, it's going to look like a tiny ice cube. You just have to get past this."

"I don't know how." I shook my head, almost dropping the phone again. "It's out there now. One Google search and the video will pop up. A video of my fat ass going down on a guy. How can I come back from that, Mav? There's no way."

"There is a way, and it involves you being strong and taking control of the narrative. This was a video taken without your consent and shared online—anyone who's viewing it should feel ashamed of themselves, and that's the point that needs to be hammered home." Maverick's frown deepened. "I've known you since we were fifteen years old. I've seen you go through so much shit, and you've always come out the other end stronger. This won't be any different."

"It will be, though." I let myself fall back against the door. The frame rattled. "This time it's beyond different."

This time, I have your little brother to think about, too.

"I'm already hiring a tech expert to scrub the video from the internet, and I've got a few lawyer friends already working on shutting down whatever sites are hosting it."

That was the first bright spot since the storm had rolled in. "Thank you, Mav. You've been helping me through this from the beginning... thank you."

More tears, except these felt a little more hopeful than the ones before. They also didn't last nearly as long.

"I'm going to pay you back for this," I promised him.

"You don't need to. I'm just looking out for you. You're family, Rex. And I would never let anyone do this to family."

Damn it. I had to tell him. This quite possibly could have been the worst time to say it, but it also could have been the best. There'd only be one way of finding out: "Maverick, something's happened since I got here. Benji and I... we've gotten close."

I tried reading his expression, but nothing shifted, nothing twitched. He waited for me to continue.

"He and I, we're together. Officially."

"Oh, whoa. Okay. Wasn't really expecting that."

Shit, maybe this really was the absolute worse time to bring it up. "Honestly, Mav, I've had feelings for him for a long, long-ass time. And since being here, we just kind of rekindled everything between us. And now, with this sex tape, now I feel like such a fucking asshole for dragging your little brother into this. Associating with me. I fucking hate it." I dropped my eyes down to the white-and-black tiled floor. "I'm sorry, Mav. I should have talked to you about it first. Maybe you could have talked me off the ledge."

"Are you kidding me?" Maverick looked insulted. "I would have told you to jump right off that ledge, headfirst."

"Huh?"

"Yeah, Rex, I would have told you to follow your heart. If I wanted anyone with my brother, I'd want someone who I knew I could trust my life in their hands with. That's you."

"So you aren't pissed off?"

"Nah," he said, waving it off. "For what? As long as you two are happy, that's really all I care about. Just don't put me in the middle of any arguments. I don't do well with that."

I chuckled, the sound surprising me. "I won't..."

"It's going to be all right, Rex. You and Benj are going to be a power couple, taking over the world one day at a time."

"I hope so... I just wish I was better for your brother. He's smart and fit and funny, and I'm here dealing with a scandal the size of my fucking waistband."

"Stop shitting on yourself, Rex. Stop." If he could

have reached through the phone screen to shake me, I'm sure he would have. "You've always been a bigger guy, and there's absolutely fucking zero that's wrong about that. Plenty of people would say the complete opposite, are you kidding me? Walk into any gay bar in a leather harness and a leather hat and you'd walk out with an entire concubine of bear-chasing gay guys. And the guys Benji's talked to in the past always had your body type, so *clearly* you're *his* type."

More laughter rose inside me, riding a wave of relief.

"It does feel like that."

"I'm sure it does." Maverick shot me some side-eye before smiling. "Benji can help you get through this, not the opposite. Trust him, and trust me when I say you're going to get through this. Stay hopeful, all right?"

I nodded, the spark of hope catching inside my chest. The world didn't seem as dark and heavy as it had before I picked up my best friend's call. The spiral slowed, stabilized. I could see a way out of this.

"Plus, there won't be any more threats," Mav said. "That's a bright side, isn't it?"

"It is, it is." I opened the bathroom door, getting hit with a draft from the open window in the hall. "I wish I knew the fucker behind this shit, though."

"Theo's still on the case, don't worry. He's not quitting until someone can be charged and prosecuted for this monstrous bullshit."

Again, more hope. It pushed away the images that flashed through my head.

A city penthouse. Twinkling lights. Three naked bodies.

"I just want this to be over with."

"I know, Rex. I know." An empathetic sadness cross through Mav's golden eyes. "It will be. Go hang out with Benji. Turn your phone off and forget about the rest of the world for now."

That was good advice, although it sounded much easier than I knew it would be. I gave an approving grunt. "I'll try," I said, already thinking about what my mom would say if she were alive right now. I knew she'd take me into her arms and tell me that it would all be all right. She loved to say "challenges are only opportunities for growth, Rex. A forest always grows greener after a fire," and she'd give me a kiss on the forehead. A magical kiss, one that took an eraser to all of my problems, making everything seem so small and inconsequential.

"All right," I said, gathering myself. "I should probably head back out, then. I don't want to worry Benji."

"And you already know he's probably nervously talking my moms' ears off. Go. Rescue all three of them."

Another laugh, and, like a rainbow after the rain, a smile. "Thanks, Mav. For everything." I choked on the word, emotion catching in my throat. "I don't know what I did to deserve a friend like you."

"You've got my back, and I've got yours. Simple as that."

"Simple as that."

We hung up and my mood felt noticeably lifted. A heavy, pregnant cloud still hung over my head, that much was sure. And I still had to deal with the fallout from this tape, which would take months, if not years to sort out. I didn't even want to think about the prospects of now pursuing a career in politics, seeing as how that was effectively shot dead with this tape.

But... still. There was hope. And maybe this was all me blowing it up in my own head. Maybe people wouldn't care as much as I assumed they would. We lived in progressive times—maybe this wouldn't be as much of a blow as I thought it was.

A blow.

Ha. Ha.

I left the bathroom, deciding that Maverick's plan really did sound like the best way to handle this. The Christmas decorations that transformed the living room into a winter wonderland helped make things feel a little bit brighter. I went to turn off my phone, ready to stuff it in a drawer and forget about it, when it started to ring.

I expected Maverick's name, which didn't show up. Another name appeared on my screen instead:

Gavin Madison.

I swiped to answer. "Hi, Dad."

23

BENJAMIN GOLD

"HEY, MA."

"Benji, come sit." Mia pulled out a chair and patted the beige cushion. She sat outside on a blanket next to the small animal house. Two volunteers sat on either side of her, Furonda with her bright smile and Tarrek with his permanent frown, both of them holding bottles for their suckling deer. My sister, Kaitlyn, was also there, wearing on old college sweatshirt that had milk spilled all down the front.

"Hey, guys." I planned on heading to my room and pacing a hole in the carpet. Rex storming away worried the hell out of me. This felt like a house of cards on the precipice of crumbling, and that scared me like nothing else. I wanted to follow him and reassure him that I couldn't give any fucks about the video. All I cared about was him, his health and his happiness. Point-blank, period.

But I didn't follow him. I did yell after him, but he didn't even slow down. He made a beeline for the guesthouse, leaving me in a wake of worry.

So maybe hanging out with my mom and some baby deer under the beaming sun would be better than going to my dark room.

I sat down across from Tarrek, who gave me a slanted smirk before turning his attention back to the deer. If I wasn't mistaken, the white mark on her side told me it was Isabella. And Tarrek handled her as if she were his own baby. There was a tenderness and care that surprised me. I didn't imagine many people seeing him out on the street, with his rugged beard and pin-up girl tattoos, would think he would be this maternal toward some orphaned animals.

"Everything okay?" my mom asked. She had a way of sensing when something was off without me ever even saying a word.

"Not really." I looked to the two volunteers and decided to be as vague as possible. "Some outside drama is really messing with Rex right now."

"I saw him rush past."

"Yeah, it's—it's pretty bad."

My mom put a hand on my shoulder, a silent move that spoke volumes. My mom's touch always comforted me, and she understood how much I needed it right now.

"I'm sure he'll be okay." I said it more so for myself than anyone else, but my mom entertained me.

"I'm sure he will, too." She waved to someone behind me.

"Look who I found at the front gate!" my mom, Ashley, called from behind. I turned and saw her walking over with Helena Ramsey at her side, another girl walking hand in hand with her.

Helena used to be a volunteer at the sanctuary for as long as I could remember. It had been a few months since she last visited, so it served as a good distraction to what currently clattered around inside my head.

"Everyone, meet my girlfriend, Leah!"

Helena stepped to the side as Leah lifted a shy hand and waved at the small group, her attention quickly pulled toward the baby deer. She squatted down so she could get a better look at the one closest to her, the typical "awws" and "ohhs" coming from her as she gently scratched the deer's head. Helena got down with her, and they both cooed at the deer, making Tarrek seem slightly uncomfortable. I noticed him grow tense, his eye contact jumping around the crowd and rarely settling.

"I'm surprised we were even let in," Helena said,

standing back up. "It's like getting into the Mint to get in here now."

Mia gave a deprecating chuckle and said, "That's what we're aiming for."

Helena's eyebrows rose. "No... The Dove?"

Both my moms nodded. The name had a toxic feel to it, tinging the air.

"But I thought they caught him."

"Yeah, we did, too," Ashley said, sighing, brushing a strand of hair back from her freckled face. "There was another threat a few weeks ago. They got Tammy."

Helena's gasp was audible. Her hands swung up to her lips, covering the scar. "Oh God, is she okay?"

"She is, she is. Shaken but okay. They broke in and shaved a dove symbol into her hair and left a note tied to her leg. Thankfully Benji and Rex found her in time. They were able to pump the poison out."

"Poison?" She looked around the yard. "Is she around?"

"I don't know—last time she was in the house. Let me see if she wants to come out and say hi." Ashley got up, spooking the deer in Tarrek's lap. He rubbed those big ears and whispered something that did the trick, Isabella calming right down and going back to emptying the bottle of milk.

Mia clapped her thighs, her frown working back

into a smile. "How've you been, Helena? We've missed you here."

"And I've missed you guys. It's been interesting, scary, fun, exciting. All the things." She grabbed Leah's hand, bringing it up to her lips. "But most of all, it's been a dream come true."

Helena had left about three years ago, dropping everything and deciding to backpack across the world. She had been dealing with some family issues, which may have caused the idea to blossom in the first place. She did seem much happier now than when I last saw her. Her hair glowed in brown waves down to her shoulders, and her smile only got bigger when Leah's hand was in hers.

"Where'd you two meet?" I asked. I threw a glance over their shoulders, to the guesthouse with the blinds drawn and door shut tight. A stab of guilt twisted in my back.

I'm going to go knock that door down if he doesn't come out in the next five minutes.

"We met in a hostel in Amsterdam. Leah's actually from Georgia—can you believe she went to our same high school, Mia?"

"No freaking way."

Leah nodded, throwing up the "Hawks fly high" hand signal— thumbs locked together and fingers wiggling. I knew it because I'd gone to the same high school.

"You two even look alike," I noted, pointing between my mom and Leah, who both had the same dark red hair, almost in the exact same style, with similar smiles and noses, too.

"You know what?" Mia said. "I was going to say something but didn't want to seem weird."

Furonda, the volunteer, nodded her head and raised her hand in agreement.

"Wait, so what year did you graduate from Hillstone?"

"Hillstone? Oh, no, I went—" Before Leah could finish, Ashley came back out, looking disappointed. She shrugged.

"I tried getting her out here. Even carried her, but she jumped off and ran back inside. I don't know what's up with her."

"Poor thing's probably still so shaken up," Helena said. "And how about River? Is the adoption still getting stalled?"

Damn, has anything good happened to us as a family recently?

River had actually been Helena's foster child for a long while, but when it was clear she couldn't care for him and after him spending time with us, it was clear what my moms planned on doing. They'd started the adoption process, and we all hoped to have a new brother before the year's end. Once the threats started rolling in, that all changed. The Dove hadn't just threatened the sanctuary, but we later found out that they threatened the adoption agency as well.

"He's doing well—I talked to him this morning actually. They moved him to a foster home down in Savannah. It's a drive, but we try to make it out as much as we can. He really wants to be here." Mia's words hitched. Mama reached over and rubbed mom's back, kissing the side of her head.

"We're hopeful," Ashley said.

"As you should be. This will all end—"

"Rex!" I jumped up, apologizing to the crowd before running around Leah and Helena, going straight for Rex. He stood just outside the door to the guesthouse, his hair a mess and his face a rosy pink, the color matching his eyes.

I ran into his open arms, wrapping mine around his.

"I'm sorry for storming off like that."

"No, what? Are you kidding me, it's fine. Are you okay?" I put my hands on either side of his face, not really caring that we were still in full view of everyone back in the yard. I couldn't imagine the pain Rex must have been feeling with such an intense violation of his personal privacy.

"I'll be okay," he said, artfully dodging the question.

"Rex, I will personally find whoever did this and throw them in a cage for the pain they're causing."

He smiled, a twisted, gnarled smile, but one nonetheless. "Theo's still on it. Just... promise you won't ever watch it, Benj."

"I would never. I swear." I leaned up and kissed him. "And anyone who is watching it is a dirty rotten pig that deserves to be shat on by a herd of flying elephants."

"Flying elephants?"

"I get creative when I'm furious."

"Ah, gotcha."

Rex's turn to kiss me. He smiled against my lips, his hands on my side.

"Besides," I said, "I've got it all in full, glorious, Rex-alicious 4-D right here."

All right, *now* I cared that we were in full view of everyone back in the yard.

"Let's go inside," I whispered. "Let's just forget about the world. You and me, let's order pizza, watch corny rom-coms, and fuck until we pass out."

Rex's eyes lit up. The worry that had been circling inside the blue depths seemed to be pushed away for a moment. He grinned and kissed me again.

"Give me two hours."

That got a brow arch out of me. "Two, huh? Where are you going?" I asked, just now realizing he had keys in his hand.

"I, uhm, talked to my father."

That made both brows leap. "You did? How did it go?"

"It went well. It was quick, but he... well, he saw the video. Or at least news of it. He told me he wants to talk to me and doesn't care about the tape. He sounded really shaken up."

"So you're gonna go?"

"I'm gonna go."

That made my heart grow a pair of wings and beat up toward the sky. This felt good, like progress was just a hug, talk, and a cry away. I knew there had been a large rift between Rex and his dad, but I could feel a bond even stronger than that. And if this bat-fucked situation ended up bringing out something good from it, then, well, *good.*

"Okay," I said, giving him another kiss. "Good luck. Call me when you get there."

"I will."

With that and one last kiss, Rex left, waving at the baby deer–feeding group. I let myself into the guest-house and flopped onto the couch, unsure exactly how this day would end.

Hopefully better than it started...

24

REX MADISON

MY DAD LIVED in a modest house in a suburb of Atlanta, on a quiet, tree-lined street with a brick front and a well-manicured lawn and hedges. I used to hate it. We moved out of our massive water-front property and into a house half its size, my dad wanting to downsize and start new after my mom passed. It marked a terrible time in my life, and the negative emotions never left me until I left this place.

The new house had always been constricting, like the colorless walls were all closing in on me. I'd ride bike only to get out of the neighborhood and onto the Silver Comet Trail, a state-crossing bike trail that offered an escape from the cookie-cutter norms that the suburbs had to offer.

Now, though, my view shifted. I thought back to the chaos of the New York city streets, the shoulder-to-shoulder mass transit, the constant smell of car exhaust and questionable body odors.

It was a contrast that I'd come to appreciate after the last few months I'd spent at the Gold Sanctuary. The quiet life sounded better and better by the day.

Things weren't going to be quiet, though. Not yet. Especially not today.

I parked next to a moving van, a sweaty pair of movers lifting up a delicate-looking wardrobe. I could see a figure monitoring them from the second-floor bedroom window, my stepmom's telltale hair bun shadowed by some kind of backlight.

I didn't bother wondering what was happening. They could remodel all they wanted. I was here to talk to my dad, and that was it.

Another pair of movers shuffled past me, holding a box of books and stacks of pamphlets. I recognized those pamphlets. They had come from Sylvia's organization, meant to "educate" about the harms of gay marriage and the prosecution those with opposing beliefs now felt.

Give me a fucking break. When you get denied seeing your dying partner at a hospital because you're missing a marriage license, then you can talk about prosecution.

It was almost enough for me to turn around and walk away. Anger seethed inside me. My father had supported her, and by extension her message, all those years. Whether he did it to collect votes or not, it didn't matter, he'd still stood behind her. And he may have not known that his own son happened to be one of the very people she shat on, but that didn't matter *either*. There were kids out there who could stumble on their toxic message and take it to heart.

My dad. Let me just talk to him and get it over with.

I couldn't imagine an explanation that would suffice, but I walked into his house with as open a heart as I could have. I thought of my mom, and how she would always lead with her heart. It never failed her, and I knew she'd want me to live the same.

The foyer was a flurry of activity. There seemed to be a few assistants both on separate calls pacing around a table full of donuts and coffee boxes. A cluster of smart-looking kids sat in a corner next to the packed bookshelf, laptops open on each of their laps. They must have been my dad's campaign team. I recognized a couple of them, from the last time my dad ran.

Only one looked my way and quickly looked back down, flustered.

They must know about the video.

I internally winced. *Of course they know about the video.*

The panic and dread tried grabbing the wheel, but somehow, someway, I managed to claw it back. I took a breath and walked up to the campaign staffer who'd looked my way. She had her dark hair braided in tight twists, falling down her shoulders, over her shirt that had my dad's name across it: Gavin Madison, the first two letters of his name capitalized with a peach underneath them, symbolizing Georgia.

"Hey, sorry, do you know where my dad is?"

"Yeah, he was outside in the backyard the last time I saw him."

"Got it, thank you."

I turned to leave, but something came over me. A burning urge that would surely come back to bite me with the force of a scorching inferno.

"I'm assuming the tape's already gotten to you guys." It sounded like someone else was speaking. I barely recognized my own voice or the words that came out. "Has my dad's chances taken a big hit?"

She adjusted her twists, throwing them over her shoulder. Her eyes told me the answer before she even spoke. "A little bit. But that's okay. I'm so sorry this even happened to you." Her eyebrows rose. "Oh, there he is!"

I turned, spotting my dad a few seconds before he spotted me.

Almost a year had passed since I'd last seen him. He hadn't changed much in that time. Still had the thick head of silvery gray hair, with a tall and imposing presence, always able to soften it with a crinkly eyed smiled. We both had the same light blue eyes and a similar build.

There were a lot of things my dad and I had that were similar, but it was what was different between us that drove the wedge.

"Dad."

"Rex."

He came over to me, and before I could even say anything else, he hugged me.

I froze, not reacting. I didn't expect this kind of reception right off the bat. This was the man who had potentially caused a six-year rift between me and the man of my dreams. He cut me off when the threats on the sex tape first started rolling in, arguably when I needed him the most. I'd been pushed away, left to defenses I wasn't sure I had.

But I did have them. And I'd made it through. The sex tape leaked and I was still standing, still breathing. Everything would be okay.

Even this.

I returned the hug, feeling my dad exhale in relief.

"Thank you for coming, son." He put a hand on my shoulder and squeezed. I saw so much of myself in his eyes, it almost scared me.

I also saw something else. A sadness dragged his gaze down, heavy bags under his eyes revealing an exhaustion that went past one or two nights of bad sleep.

"Come, let's go into my office."

I followed my dad through an emptying living room. The couch was barely visible behind the stack of cardboard boxes, all labeled with thick black marker in a hasty script on loosely taped labels.

"You guys moving out?" I asked.

"I'm not."

I looked to him in surprise.

"Come inside, I'll explain."

He opened the door into his office, a room I'd always found to be a cozy and homey escape. I remembered being a little kid and sneaking into his office just so I could play my Game Boy on his big comfortable leather chair, next to the window that looked out onto the vegetable garden in the backyard.

The office remained the same as it had all those years ago, with the same leather chair propped against the corner of the wall, next to the round porthole window that had been the catalyst to so many of my daydreams as a kid.

I went straight for the chair and sat, the leather cushion feeling like memory foam as it hugged me like it had all those years ago. My dad stood, leaning on his desk, his arms crossed. He wore a simple gray T-shirt that could use a pass or two under a steamer, and a pair of equally wrinkled jeans.

That was also pretty atypical of my dad, who normally wore pressed suits and tailored polos everywhere he went.

"So," I started. "A lot's happened…"

"Rex, you don't have to explain anything about that tape."

"I know, but I feel like I need to apologize? I don't know—"

"No, no. That's not why I called you here. I don't ever want to hear you apologize for being violated the way you were. You were a victim, Rex. A sorry should never come from your mouth." He rubbed the back of his neck, gaze dropping again. "Me, on the other hand." He lifted his eyes back to mine. "I'm the one who needs to apologize. I'm so sorry, Rex. I failed you as a father, and I'm so desperately sorry for that."

"Dad, you didn't fail me. Just because I'm bi—"

"That's not what I mean. I failed you by not being there when you needed me the most. I should have dropped everything and flown out to New York as soon as the threat landed in my email. I should have been there for you, my own son. And I failed."

"Dad—"

"Not only did I fail, but I was lying the entire time.

Living a fabricated self, destroying my own flesh and blood in the process."

I cocked my head. "What do you mean?"

"You know your grandparents, how religious they were. It was so hard living in that environment, feeling like you woke up and your very existence was a sin, only because of who you found attractive. I couldn't do it. I stuffed it all down. It worked. For a little bit, but that's only ever like putting a piece of tape on a cracked dam. It might stop some of the trickle, but that thing's going to blow eventually."

"Dad..."

"I married your mom, and I loved her, I really, really loved her." He started to cry then. "And we had you, and I felt like my life was complete. Everything I ever wanted, I had." He took in a breath, barely pulling himself together, and it made me start to come undone, my bottom lip trembling. I'd only ever seen my dad like this once before.

At my mom's funeral.

"But I didn't. Deep down, I knew something would always be missing. A light switch that needed to be flipped before I could truly see, ever really be happy." He put his hands to his chest. "I'm flipping that switch, son. I'm turning on the light, and I'm coming out of the dark: Rex, I'm gay."

That shocked me. An electric bolt right to the chest. I stammered for words before settling on "Wow. *Wow.*" And then a few seconds later, "Come here." I stood and opened my arms, all the crap I'd felt between me and my dad disappearing in an instant. This moment catapulted us past all the bullshit, into entirely new territory.

"I love you, Dad." I said, embracing him tightly— still completely shell-shocked, but beginning to feel a huge shift happening between my dad and me.

"Jeez, I've been wanting to say that for so long." My dad's smile seemed shades brighter, his eyes filled with a fresh light. "Is it always that nerve-racking?"

"It gets a little easier. It does." I rubbed my face, having a hard time believing the turn of events. "Is that why you've been calling?"

My dad nodded. "It wasn't something I could have ever done over text."

"Fuck. I feel like such a dick."

"Don't—I understand. We needed to work our way here, but I'm really glad we did."

"So, I'm guessing Sylvia knows this, too?"

My dad nodded, his eyes doing a slight roll. "She was the catalyst. When she emptied your bank account—"

"Wait, wait, that wasn't you?"

"No." My dad's face was a picture of honesty. He may have been a career politician, but I'd grown up under his wing long enough to know when he told the truth or painted it with an exaggeration or two. "That's the other reason I wanted to talk to you. After I received that email with the threat, I left my laptop open and she read it. She saw what was coming, and since she has access to the accounts, she transferred everything out of it. I wasn't keeping a close eye on it—I don't like to feel like I'm keeping track of you—so I didn't notice until recently. That's when I shifted everything back. And it's when I told her I wanted a divorce."

"Holy shit... I thought— This entire time. Fuck."

"It's okay. It's all in the past, now."

"But what about your Senate seat? This is... I mean, it's going to cause some waves."

My dad huffed a laugh and said, "A tidal wave." He seemed a little more relaxed now that his burden had been lifted. "I'm ready for it. I've been working on a speech for weeks now, and I think I've got it done. There was just one thing left: Rex, son, do you want to stand on the stage with me? It'll be televised, and I know you hate that kind of attention, so I'm okay with you sayin—"

"I'll do it." I answered before I could even second-guess it. "Let me know when and where."

"Thank you, Rex." My dad took me into another hug, and this time I wasn't so slow with returning it.

Before I could fully totally okay about this reunion, there was one more question I needed to ask. Something that had been sticking in my side like a splinter.

"Dad, back when I was younger, six years ago, I went on a trip to Costa Rica."

"Yeah, I remember, with the Golds."

"Yup," I said, hoping this next question didn't undo all the progress we'd just managed to make. "You bought me a phone for that trip. Benji and I, we were getting close, until he got a text telling him basically to fuck off. It came from my phone, but I know I never sent it... Did you?"

"No, I would never—"

"Sylvia?"

My dad took a moment before nodding in agreement. "Sylvia. She bought the phone. She must have had some kind of way to read and reply to your messages. Fucking shit. I thought she did it to be kind, to win you over a little. I didn't know she was spying on you." I could see my dad's face shift into a red hue. He was never one to get angry, but today definitely seemed different.

"It's all right, Dad. She may have tried to stop us, but true love can't get cock-blocked forever, especially not by a woman with a haircut that belongs in one of those black-and-white hairdressers books from the nineties."

My dad laughed loud at that one.

"You two are together?" he asked.

"We are," I said, my smile growing wider. "I guess I have her to thank for breaking us apart that first time, but also for pushing us back together this second time. If she never emptied my bank account, I may have stayed in my little dazed-out existence up in New York. Weird to say, but, well, I guess I'm grateful that Sylvia is such a raging cu—"

"No, no! The suitcases with my clothes go *before* the boxes with my shoes. Rodrigo, listen to me!" Sylvia's voice drifted to nothingness as she hounded the movers out into the front lawn.

My dad and I looked to each other and couldn't help but laugh again. It felt like being a kid again, my dad finding me in his office after falling asleep with a book on my chest. Sometimes he'd carry me off to bed when I was too grumpy and sleep-addled to move myself, always tucking me in exactly the way I liked. My mom would come in shortly after and give me a kiss on the forehead, the last but very vital ingredient to a perfect night's sleep.

I stayed in my dad's office for a couple more hours, sinking into the leather chair and slipping back into the old days.

25

BENJAMIN GOLD

KAITLYN and I sat in the kitchen after cleaning up from dinner. A stack of clean dishes sat on a checkered towel, ready to be put away. At my feet, Penelope sat chewing on a bone with Tammy curled up under a sheet of her golden fur. I put a foot on Penelope's back and rubbed, looking to my sister. She pushed a steaming hot cup of coffee my way which I gratefully thanked her for. It had been a hell of a day, and some extra-strong coffee was exactly what I needed.

"Any word from Rex?"

"Nothing," I said, taking a long sip. The warmth coated my throat, spreading through me and waking me up with a jolt.

"I'm sure he's okay." Kaitlyn's hopeful smile kept my mood lifted, even though anxiety still coiled inside me like a viper ready to strike, hungry to sink its fangs in a deadly bite.

I took another sip of coffee before saying, "I hope so. Not only did that fucking video leak, but I just don't know how his dad would take the news. I've tried calling him, but it goes to voicemail."

Kaitlyn curled a strand of brown hair around her finger. "I'm sure he just got tired of all the noise and turned off his phone. I don't blame him."

"Neither do I. I'm just worried."

"I know, Benj, I know." She reached across the table and put her hand on mine. My sister had been one of the first people to find out that Rex and I were together, and she had taken the news with as much grace and poise as someone who already knew the sky was blue and the grass green. She clearly had seen it coming from miles away, which made me wonder why Rex and I were the only ones who got the message late?

"How 'bout you, Kate? What's stressing you out today?"

My sister chuckled and sat back in the chair, the wood creaking. She shrugged and looked out the window. "My plate is nothing compared to yours. I'm just stressed about finding an apartment right now."

My sister was a traveling nurse and usually bounced from spot to spot. It meant I had gone some months without seeing her, so it was nice to have her home for a week or two while she finalized her next steps.

"I'm sure you'll find one," I said, reassuring her. "You're going to LA, not the Amazon."

She laughed at that, loud enough to spook Penelope. "That is true. Although I wouldn't mind having a job in the Amazon. I feel like I'd come back with so many stories."

"Yeah, and so many leeches, too."

"I'm not going to get in the water, Benj."

I cocked my head. "Knowing you, that's the first thing you'd do."

She laughed again, nodding. My sister had always been adventurous, more so than me or Maverick. Dusty *definitely* wasn't one for big adventures, so it usually fell on me, Kate, and Mav to venture off and explore the edges of whatever playground or forest we were in, reporting back to Dusty with whatever we stumbled on.

The door opened then. I sat up, expecting to see one of my moms walking in, or a volunteer coming to check out. It was already late in the day, and now was usually the time they left, although one or two still stuck around.

Rex walked in, a heavy-looking bag slung over his shoulder. I stood up, relieved to see a grin spread across his face. I had worried that he'd be just as upset as he'd been when he left hours earlier, or worse.

"Hey there," he said as I hurried up to him, kissing him and feeling that delicious scratch of his beard against my chin.

"I've been worried, Rex."

"I know, I'm sorry. I turned my phone off."

"That's fine, totally fine." I held both his hands in mine. Even though I'd been home this entire time, it wasn't until now that I felt comfortable. Like I'd been the one to walk through those doors after been years away (even though it had only been a few hours... I could be dramatic every now and then, all right?).

"What's in the bag?"

"All my regrets and fears and doubts."

"Looks heavy."

"I had a *fuckton* of regrets and fears and doubts." He smiled and kissed me again, the tips of our noses brushing together. "Come with me. Let's go dump them in a lake and watch them sink."

"Sounds like a plan," I said. We said bye to my sister, who had been focused on scrolling through her phone in an obvious attempt to give us some privacy.

We walked out of the house, and instead of heading toward the guesthouse, Rex grabbed my hand and led us to the stables. "What's really in the bag?" I asked.

"You'll find out," he said, a playful tone sparking in his voice.

"Another surprise."

"Another one."

He let go of my hand, only so that he could give me a playful spank. I jumped, the jolt of his hand on my ass making me tingly.

"Saddle up Canyon. I've got Electra." Rex went to work saddling Electra, who seemed just as happy to have Rex's attention as I did. She batted those miles-long lashes and playfully nipped at Rex's shirt, her tail swinging back and forth in a more-than-relaxed manner. I finished up with Canyon and hopped on, following Rex as he and Electra clopped out of the stable and onto the trail that wound off the sanctuary grounds and around the back.

"So what happened?" I said, spurring Canyon on to move a little faster so we trotted side by side. I tried keeping my tone neutral, but I'd been dying to know how his meeting with his dad had gone for hours now.

"We talked and we really made a ton of progress. Everything he told me sounded genuine and sincere, and I really believed him." Rex looked over at me, his smile wide. "He came out to me, Benj. He's gay. And he's been eaten up about keeping it a secret for so long. He's making a big speech about it this week, and he's dedicating the rest of his career for pushing LGBTQ rights and equality."

If I were driving a car, I may have steered it off the road in surprise.

Thankfully, Canyon had more of a brain to navigate when I started to go haywire.

"Whoa," I said. "That's... wow."

"Yeah, pretty much my same reaction. I don't think I ever saw it coming, but now that it's out there, I kinda see hints of it from our past. Hindsight is twenty-twenty, but still, there were hints."

"And how are you feeling?"

"About my dad?"

I looked ahead, to the leaf-covered path. "About everything." I didn't even want to bring up the sex tape, scared to hurt Rex by simply mentioning it.

"I'm feeling better," he said, his chin held high. "I think the initial shock is wearing off. I haven't looked at my phone at all, and it feels kind of liberating. Obviously, shit's still out there, but I spoke to your brother, and he said he's already hired someone to scrub the internet for it."

"Jeez, Mav, what a hero that guy is."

"He really, really is. I owe him a lot." He looked to me as our horses turned, going down the narrow tree-lined path I had shown him earlier. "I told him about us, too."

"You did? How'd he take it?" My heart started to beat a little harder. I loved my big brother, and I really valued his judgment and opinions. If he reacted negatively toward us, then—

"He was great about it."

Oh thank God.

"Huh?"

"Oh. I, uh—" *Didn't realize I spoke out loud.* "I said 'thank God.'"

Rex chuckled and nodded, agreeing with me. "I didn't expect him to blow up or anything, but still, he's my best friend and you're his little brother—it definitely had the potential of getting messy."

"Mav is the king of mess. He probably feeds off it. Have you ever seen his room? His refrigerator? His *hamper*?" I shivered, thinking back to the times we all lived under the same roof. Even though he had a successful and glitzy life in New York City, it didn't mean that my brother had changed very much from the sloppy but gold-hearted guy who had everyone else's best interests at heart over his own.

"I've seen way more than I ever should see," Rex said. "And I agree, he's probably more happy about the news than anyone else."

"Probably," I said, smiling. That pretty much meant my entire family knew about me and Rex, the only ones I really cared about. They all knew and they were all happy about it, making *me* even happier. There had been plenty of road bumps getting here (one of those road bumps lasting an entire six freaking years), but at least we got here.

"We're here," Rex said, reading my mind, as the trees opened around us and the sound of the small waterfall filled the air. A gentle mist floated through the darkening sky, the sun already setting, having moved down past the tree line. He tied Electra to the same tree as before. He dropped the heavy bag on the floor and unzipped it while I got Canyon settled in and secured.

"Oh, and get this." Rex started to pull out a thick blue blanket from the bag. "Sylvia, my dad's wife— well, *ex-wife* now—was the one responsible for that text message. The one you got in Costa Rica. She'd been the one to buy me that phone, and she had rigged it so she could see and respond to my messages. She saw our texts and replied, deleting it on my end so I never even knew what she sent you."

"Are you—what the fuck. Seriously?"

"Seriously. And she did something similar when she went around my father's back and emptied out my bank accounts."

"Wow, that is *evil*."

Rex nodded, shrugging. "Thankfully, my dad came to his senses and filed for divorce. It's going to be a really hard road to reelection, but I already see him a thousand times happier. Plus—" He smiled at me as he took out a set of candles, setting them on the corners of the massive blanket. "—I managed to switch the labels on all of her boxes and loosened up a few of them from the bottom. She's going to have an interesting time unpacking."

That had me cracking up. "Oh man, that's going to make her move so much more hellish." I lifted a hand, and Rex met it with a slap. "Nice." And then I leaned in to kiss those big lips, both of us smiling as I almost pushed Rex onto the blanket. He managed to stay up and finished emptying his backpack, pulling out a lantern that crackled to life when he lit it and set it on the side, near the river's gently rolling edge. Next, he brought out a plate of chocolate-covered strawberries and a bottle of champagne, with two well-wrapped glasses.

"Jeez, it's like watching Mary Poppins after she put the kids down to sleep."

Rex gave a loud belly laugh.

"Any other goodies in there?" I said, looking in and expecting to see an entire damn elephant looking back at me.

"That's it," Rex said, lifting the champagne and popping the cork. Golden bubbles fizzed upward, the foam dripping down the side of the black bottle. He poured a healthy amount into one flute and then the other, before handing me a glass.

"Cheers," he said, "to new beginnings after second chances."

"And to Karma diligently working her magic on heartless bitches."

"Cheers to that, too." Our glasses clinked together, and I drank the bubbly drink, an instant buzz working itself up through my body. I set the glass on a smooth patch of grass and leaned in, putting a hand on Rex's knee. It was getting dark, but the sky above was beginning to blink to life with a field of stars shining through. The moon, hanging full and bright, added to the light, almost making the candles and lantern unnecessary.

They did add some really sexy vibes, though, and I wasn't complaining about that one bit.

"This was such a great idea," I said. Rex picked up a strawberry, but instead of bringing it to his own lips, he brought it to mine. I leaned in and took a bite, smiling as I chewed. He took the rest of it, leaving a little tuft of green between his fingers.

"It reminds me a little of our Costa Rican trip. Now *that* was an escape. I needed something similar after today."

I looked around, envisioning the tall Costa Rican canopy taking the place of the dwarfed-by-comparison woods of Georgia. Instead of the birds chirping, we'd be hearing monkeys howling and singing, the air thick with humidity and possibility, sparking with the same energy that electrified the space between us.

"It's like that night."

Rex, kissing me, spoke against my lips. "That velvet midnight. I'll never forget it."

"Never," I said, kissing him back, this time successful at pushing him down onto the blanket.

26

REX MADISON

SIX YEARS AGO

"I DON'T THINK I'm ever forgetting this night," Benji said, lying down next to me as we looked up at the Costa Rican jungle, an almost surreal sight. It felt so alien, the trees stretching up toward the stars, a huge difference from the trees in my backyard.

Everything about this trip was different. Was it being so far from home that did it? Or was it Benjamin Gold, the guy who could get my heart skipping beats with a smirk and a few blinks of his long lashes?

Not even winks. He didn't have to wink. Blinks were fine. Anything was fine when it came to Benji. He could chew his toenails off with his teeth and I'd probably still find that attractive about him. I couldn't explain it exactly—I just felt it, down deep in the center of my chest. Everything about Benji was just *right*.

Tonight was our last night before going back to the real world, and I wanted to enjoy every second of it.

So I asked Benji if he wanted to spend the night in a tree house that had been built by the owners of the primate sanctuary. Normally it was supposed to be used for events or paid renters, but I managed to sweet-talk my way into borrowing it for the night.

Benji had seemed really excited when I'd brought it up to him. We didn't want to bring up any questions about the two of us spending the night together, so we agreed to wait until everyone was asleep. We snuck out and made our way to the tree house, climbing up the rickety steps and settling into the large room.

It was built like a studio apartment, as one large room with a comfortable bed and a small couch, along with a tiny dresser and a mirror up against one of the wooden walls. There were windows all around and a glass moonroof that looked up at a star-blotted sky.

I wasn't sure at exactly what point it was, but we found ourself in the bed, lying down, facing up and looking through the clear glass at the midnight sky.

"I'm never forgetting this trip," I said, looking over at Benji. "I've learned so much. And not just about primate conservation either. I've learned a lot about myself."

"Oh, really?"

"Yeah. A hell of a lot."

Benji leaned up on the bed. There was only one light in the tree house, but we had turned that off pretty early in the night. There was plenty of light coming in from above to let us see every little detail.

"Like...?"

"Well—" Should have seen that coming. Benji liked to dig. "—just about how I feel with certain things."

"Okay." He cocked his head and smiled mischievously. "Like...?"

We both laughed. Benji dropped his head, which made it land in the crook of my arm. He still laughed, but even with the laughter died down, he didn't move his head.

And my arm remained frozen. Scared that even a twitch of a muscle would scare him off, like some rare butterfly landing on my arm.

"I realized I'm fine without always having working electricity or hot water. I realized I'm not a huge fan of an all-veggie diet. I realized I'm fucking pissed off at the amount of deforestation happening and the effect it's having on these poor animals." I took a breath, looking up through the glass. "And, I realized, I'm not straight. Not with the way I feel about you."

The air seemed to get sucked out of the room. I couldn't tell if Benji was upset or shocked or angry or happy or—

"I feel the same way, about you. I mean, I've known I'm gay for years now, but I've also just realized that you and me... we're a really good match. Like *really* good."

"*Really* fucking good," I said, laughing in agreement. He had moved closer, his body pressing up against me so that I could feel every curve, every ridge, every twitch.

"We just click," I said, letting my heart speak instead of my brain. "I feel like I have a blast every single time I'm around you. And everything feels so *easy*. I think that's the thing about us. Life just doesn't seem so hard when you're around." I looked away from the stars, into the galaxy of Benji's gaze.

"It's the same for me," he said. "I don't stress about the stupid stuff when you're around. And we're always laughing. And you're always teaching me something. It just flows."

"It flows."

"I've been waiting for this," he said, eyes looking into mine.

"Really?" I asked. It was a surprise to me. We'd been flirty through this trip, for sure, but I hadn't known he felt anything before now.

Like I had.

"Yeah." He chewed on his bottom lip. "I just figured you were pretty much off-limits. I thought, you know, you were straight. And you're Mav's best friend. I always had my eyes on you, but it was more a fantasy than anything else."

"Damn," I said, "and I'd been fantasizing about you, too."

"So much wasted time."

"Think we can make up for some of it?"

Benji nodded, his smile turning into a wicked grin that lit a bonfire, flames spreading through my veins.

"I think we can try," I said, teasing him now. Something between us had shifted, and it wasn't just our erections. This moment felt consequential. Like there'd be absolutely no coming back from this.

And I didn't care. I knew I didn't want to come back from this. I wanted it all.

I wanted Benjamin Gold.

Before I knew what was happening, I leaned in and kissed my best friend's little brother, crashing through a barrier that had no chance of holding the two of us back. We had a magnetic pull that felt undeniable.

The kiss cracked a whip inside me. I pushed my fingers through his hair, directing the kiss into something more, something stronger.

"A velvet midnight," I said, breathless. The questioning look in his eyes made me motion up through the skylight.

"It's a velvet midnight. My mom would say that only magic happens on nights that the sky looks like this. Like a velvet sheet of stars from edge to edge."

"Let's make some magic, then," Benji said, his hands coming up to my face and his lips meeting mine again, locking together, bodies twining.

***

THE KISS FELT SAVAGE. Hungry. Primal.

Benji's tongue wrapped around mine, lips locked and bodies pressed against each other even tighter. I thrust my hips upward, rubbing myself on him, swallowing the needy moan he gave me. He tasted like strawberries and sex and midnight stars all swirled into a perfect mix. I could smell the dirt and grass and water in the air mixing with Benji's scent, creating another intoxicating mixture.

"God," I said into Benji's mouth, "I need this. You. So bad." He bit my lip, I sucked on his.

"Me too" was all he could say before our kiss exploded, expanded. I started to suck on his neck, Benji throwing his head back and moaning up into the night sky. My hands slipped under his shirt, feeling his soft skin, the hard rise and fall of the muscles underneath. His heat flowing through my palm matched the inferno that burned inside my own core.

"I need you, baby." I took his shirt off as I spoke, throwing it into the grass.

Benji responded with another moan, our erections rubbing over the other through our pants. If it got any hotter between us, I didn't think we'd have any clothes left to go back with.

Better take them all off, then.

I got to work, unzipping my jeans, Benji following my lead. He stood up and kicked off his pants. We were so far off the main trail that I didn't imagine anyone coming to find us, especially not at this time of night.

I pulled off my pants and threw them in Benji's pile. Shirt next. Then, the only thing left for either of us was our tented briefs. Benji stood above me, his body shining underneath the moonlight, the flickering candles adding a mesmerizing depth. He looked like an oil painting brought to life.

"Fuck, Rex." He looked down at me and stroked himself over his briefs, the wet stain growing. The burning want in his eyes drove me wild. He needed me, that much was clear. Now I wanted to show Benji how much I needed *him*.

I took off my underwear, my hard cock flopping out onto my stomach. I spit in my hand and stroked, looking up at him with love-drunk eyes, my hard dick leaking from how badly I wanted him. I opened my legs a little wider and rubbed my chest, my stomach, my nipples.

Then I moved my hands between my legs, underneath me. Benji watched with his lips half-parted, his cock now out through the leg of his briefs. He stroked harder, pushing aside his briefs. The tip of him glinted wet under the orange candlelight.

I spit in my hand again and brought my fingers down to my hole, rubbing myself for him. He stared with wide, lusty eyes.

"Come down here," I said, teasing my hole open but wanting something besides my own fingers.

Lucky for me, Benji had exactly what I was looking for.

I reached into the backpack and brought out a pack of lube. We'd both gotten tested after making it official, so I felt we didn't need condoms tonight. I tore the packet open and poured it on my hand before rubbing it on Benji's thick, veiny cock. He closed his eyes and moaned as I stroked, admiring the heat that poured off him.

I lay back down and pushed two fingers inside, getting myself ready for him.

"Fuck, Rex, you don't understand how fucking hot you are."

"No, no I don't," I said, giving a self-deprecating laugh, mixing with a moan as I pulled out.

Benji leaned down, his hands rubbing up and down my body, worshipping every single one of the curves. He squeezed my chest, his fingers twisting around my pebbled nipples. He bent down and licked, taking one between his lips, sucking and rolling, then moving on to the next, making my cock throb with each swirl of his tongue.

"Get inside me," I growled against the top of his head. "Please."

The head of his cock pressed against me. All he need to do was *push*. I was ready, my body practically crying out for him.

And then he pushed, his cock opening me and slipping inside. The stretch was barely there, my body already so hungry for him that he fit perfectly inside. He thrust, sinking himself deep and yanking a cry from the both of us, pleasure mixed with drunk lust. I gripped his shoulder and begged him to go harder, to give it to me, to make me shout even louder.

He did. He thrust and drove his cock balls-deep. My legs shook in the air, my body quaking with every fuck. I looked up, into his eyes, then past him, up to the silky white expanse of stars that blanketed the sky.

"That's it, oh fuck, Benji, fuck!"

He started to slow, his rhythm finding a softer beat. He thrust forward before sliding almost all the way out, his eyes focused down between my legs. I grabbed my balls and worked them, scared of touching my dick and spontaneously busting. I was already so close. Just a few more strokes, just a few—

Wait, why was he stopping.

"Why are you stopping?"

Benji slowly pulled out completely, leaving me with that burning hunger that cried out to be filled. He looked into my eyes with that greedy lust lighting up his pupils.

"Let's flip," he said. "I want you to bottom for you."

Well, guess it was my turn for a surprise.

27

BENJAMIN GOLD

"LET'S FLIP. I want to bottom for you."

I said it before I could rethink it. Not that I was able to form many coherent thoughts anyway. Not with Rex's heat wrapped tight around me.

Rex's eyes sparked with lightning. He growled as I pulled out of him, his cock twitching, thick and long. A pang of nerves hit me in the gut. I hadn't bottomed for anyone before, and Rex didn't exactly have a "starter dick kit" hanging between his legs. It was very much the opposite. Way bigger than the one or two fingers I've had inside me before.

Way, way bigger.

I took a breath. We readjusted on the blanket, Rex lying down on his back, holding his cock by the base, aiming it up. I grabbed the lube and wasn't shy about squirting it on, applying a *very* generous amount. Rex twitched as I stroked, smiling in a lusty kind of way. He looked at me in a way that foreshadowed what was to come, his blue gaze sizzling with heat.

"Fuck, baby," Rex said, eyes looking me up and down as I stood above him. "I can stay under you all fucking night."

"Good." I squatted down, reaching behind me and grabbing his pulsing cock. I lined it up with my hole, using my other arm to hold myself up, the grass and dirt wet under my palm.

Rex massaged me as I slowly lowered myself onto him. *Slowly* being the key word.

The moment he pushed into me, I felt a sharp sting. A short gasp accompanied the shock of it. Rex froze, looking up into my eyes. The sting didn't grow or turn into anything else but a distant echo. My dick pulsed in the air and oozed a string of precome down onto Rex's hairy belly.

I squatted deeper, no longer feeling a sting. Instead, an intense pressure began to build, getting stronger with the more of Rex I took inside. I took a deep breath, remembering to relax.

"Fuck, Benj. Your hole's so fucking tight."

I licked my lips, his words driving me down further. The stretch became more pronounced, the pleasure rising with it. I looked down, thinking I was already sitting on his lap and not realizing I still had about halfway to go.

Rex started pushing upward, lifting himself off the blanket, driving his lubed cock in deeper. He met barely any resistance. I moaned as he massaged my inner walls, pulling out before pushing back in, halfway, further, further.

I closed my eyes and sat down fully, impaling myself on him. My fingers dug for purchase in the ground, dirt scraping underneath my fingernails. I cried out as Rex thrust deeper, hitting my P-spot, making a galaxy of stars explode across my vision.

"Keep going," I urged, squatting so that he had space to thrust up, fucking me. My hands went onto his chest, and I held myself there, looking down into a pair of blue gems, half-lidded with ecstasy. Rex's grip tightened around my hips.

I became comfortable, no longer fearing anything about being with Rex. I started to bounce down on him, taking the reins and riding his cock, rolling my hips so that I could feel him hit every fucking inch of me.

My dick slapped against Rex, hard and leaking, my balls tightening with every rock of my hips. For someone who'd never ridden a dick before, judging by how Rex's eyes were rolling back, I didn't think I was doing a half-bad job.

I leaned forward, Rex grabbing the momentum back and thrusting into me. Our animalistic grunts and skin slapping mingled with the chorus of cicadas and scattered hoots of an owl. I sucked Rex's bottom lip between my teeth, licking and nibbling and moaning as he continued to fill me.

"Oh, Rex, right there. God that feels so good. Fuck, keep going, keep going."

I urged him on, burying my head in his neck as he rammed into me. His teeth clamped on my shoulder and bit down, the jolt of pain blending together with the rush of bliss.

"I'm getting so fucking close," I warned. The point of no return was coming at me with the force of a freight train.

I leaned back up, the movement lining his cock up perfectly with my swollen prostate. I sat back, bouncing up and down, hitting my spot over and over and over and ov—

"Oh fuck, fuck." I grabbed my dick right as the moment washed over me in a tidal wave. I shot blast after blast of come, Rex continuing to fuck it out of me. I emptied with every deep thrust he gave me.

Before my climax ended, he started to tense underneath me. I leaned back, taking in all of him. He shut his eyes and snapped his hands around my sides as he unloaded inside me. He filled me with his heat, and I watched as the pink flush rose through his chest, spreading across his neck and cheeks.

Our heavy breathing joined the mix of sounds. I leaned back down, Rex's cock still inside me. I kissed him, smiling against his lips. He playfully licked me, his grin just as wide as mine. His hands made soft circles on my back, and I could feel his heart beating against mine.

If I could wrap us up in amber and preserve this moment for the rest of eternity, I would have done it in a single synced-up heartbeat. Everything about tonight felt perfect, and considering the events that led up to tonight, it only made that "perfect" feeling even sweeter.

I moved off Rex, his cock popping out of me with some of his come dripping between my legs. I collapsed on the blanket, my entire body spent. Rex got comfortable next to me on the blanket, our bodies seeming to touch at every possible spot. My toes curled and my body twitched when Rex's leg brushed against my softening dick.

"That was fucking incredible," I said, smiling up into the field of stars.

"I didn't know you were such a power bottom."

"Neither did I." I laughed and playfully slapped Rex's chest. "You bring it out of me."

"Funny," Rex said. "I think I'm lying in a puddle of something else I brought out of you."

"Whoops," I replied, laughing and cuddling into Rex's side. I put a hand over his chest and played with the dark hair, rubbing him up and down. His heart beat against my ear, a rhythmic *lub dub* that held a hypnotizing quality.

"This was such a great idea," I said. The candle and lantern light threw a wide space of flickering orange light onto the peaceful scene, the full moon lighting up the rest. Electra and Canyon both stood next to their trees, seeming as relaxed as the two of us. A gentle, delicate spray from the nearby waterfall rose through the air, brushing over us like passing clouds.

"I need this. Needed you."

"Whenever you need me, I'm here for you. Whenever."

Rex pressed his soft lips against my forehead. He kissed me, the warmth in my body no longer focused on my come-filled ass. The heat exploded outward, and I felt carried up into space, as if I'd hopped on a hot-air balloon designed by NASA.

"You know," Rex said, looking back up at the night sky, "I really did think that tape leaking would be the

end of it for me. I thought it would just be game over."
Rex shook his head, turning to look into my eyes. "It
wasn't. Not at all. The people closest to me understand
what happened, and anyone else who wants to judge
can go fuck right off. It doesn't matter. None of it
does."

It made me happy, listening to Rex regaining
control.

"I feel like everything's falling into place, even
though earlier today it felt like it was all falling apart.
I've got my relationship with my dad back, and I've got
you, here, underneath another velvet midnight."

I swallowed, remembering that star-covered Costa
Rican sky.

Remembering how strongly I had felt for Rex, even
back then, when it felt like such an impossibility. Sure,
I had let myself drift into a hopeful dreamscape where
we'd come back to Georgia and walk off hand in hand
into the big gay rainbow sunset.

When I got that text, basically saying that I was a
mistake to him, it shattered the dreamscape and
brought me right back down to reality.

Well, at least what I assumed reality to be at the
time.

It took out all the wind from my sails, and I had
given up on any hope we would work. Once he moved
to New York, I had figured it was dead and done. And,

although I'd occasionally find myself drifting back into the colorful dreamscape, I *never* imagined that we'd be in this position, lying naked with each other underneath another velvet midnight, with plenty more seemingly lined up.

"Benji," Rex said, in that tone that told me something big was coming around the corner. I sat up, perched on his chest, looking down into his sparkling blue eyes. They reflected some of the moonlight, casting a magical glow. "I love you."

The words swirled in the air like a spell, almost knocking me out.

I blinked, speechless.

Rex kept going, barreling forward. "I do. I'm in love with you, Benji. You've taught me so much, not only about loving myself, but also about life, about taking a situation and turning it around, into something better, brighter. You always make me laugh, and you're always running through my dreams. For six years, you never stopped visiting me in my dreams. I never imagined my dreams coming true, but they have. And I don't ever want to lose you again." He kissed me, shocking my heart back into beating. "I love you, Benjamin Gold. Like nothing else in this world."

Not sure when, but at some point, I started to cry. I wiped at my tears, grateful for them. "These are happy tears," I said, hoping to ease Rex's worried expression.

"Rex, I fell in love with you from the moment we met. I can't even explain it. But I was sure of it. Just like I'm sure of it, now. And you helped me reach the point where I can even *feel* love again. When you first got here, I wasn't feeling anything at all. Everything was painted in shades of gray. I really did think I was supposed to live the rest of my life like that. Then I got sparks of color breaking through, all because of you. I started to remember how electrifying life actually felt, and I realized I wasn't meant to live in the gray. I got the help I needed, and I can cry happy tears again. I love you, Rex. So freaking much."

We kissed again, and I felt as if wings had sprouted from my shoulders. I shut my eyes and envisioned us drifting through the milky-white expanse of stars and moons and planets, swirling around comets and twirling underneath asteroids, holding hands as we flew through the rocky rings of Saturn, our souls joined as one while we explored the endless reaches of the universe.

That's how it felt kissing Rex, professing my love to him underneath that velvet midnight. We had come such a long way from the lost and confused souls we met as. Maybe it all happened exactly as it was supposed to, then. Maybe no other path would have lead to this exact moment, a moment I would never forget, not for the rest of my life or for whatever came after.

"I love you," I said again, against his lips, the words tasting as sweet as the elixir of life on my tongue.

"Forever," Rex replied, a response that would indeed last us *forever*.

MY DAD WORKED a crop circle into the beige carpet of the hotel room. His eyes were glued to the paper in his hands, his two aides sitting on the round table next to the window, scrolling through their phones for any last-minute updates. I sat on the couch with Benji, going over my speech one last time. I felt nervous, but unlike my dad, I found that I could contain it a little better.

Although my constantly bouncing leg would probably argue the opposite.

"One more time?" Benji asked, flipping the page over so we could start from the beginning.

I shook my head. "No, I think I've got it."

"I'm sure you do."

I leaned in for a reassuring kiss. I never got tired of

Benji's kisses. We could be on a sinking submarine, heading down to the ocean floor, and just one kiss from Benji would float us right back up to the surface. He was my everything, and I felt like the luckiest guy in the world whenever his lips were on mine.

Today was no different.

Well, maybe it was *a little* different.

"Dad, how ya feeling?" I looked to my father, who wore a sharp suit, his pants pressed and his light blue shirt ironed to within a thread of its life.

"I'm feeling all right. These things always give me the heebie-jeebies."

"I think you might be the only one who still says heebie-jeebies."

"Sorry, sorry. What's the trending phrase, then? Jeebie-heebies?"

Benji and I both laughed. "Yeah, sure, go with that."

My dad gave a sarcastic smile and got back to looking at the sheet of paper. A cool spring breeze floated in through the open windows, the bird of paradise plant next to the couch rustling in the wind.

"How 'bout you?" I asked, turning my attention to my boyfriend. He looked so fucking handsome today (and every day for that matter). The dark blue shirt he wore made his light eyes pop, and his fresh fade haircut made his strong brows and jaw even more prominent, drawing my eyes to his perfect lips.

Those lips curled into a soft smile. "I'm not the one who's about to be onstage."

That's what you think.

"And your test?" I asked, keeping my thoughts to myself. I focused on keeping my leg still. My nerves felt frayed, and it wasn't just because I was supposed to take the stage with my dad today at the GLAAD Awards. Although that in itself was nerve-racking as all fuck, especially thinking about all the big names in the crowd and all the people watching at home. But there was something even bigger on the horizon that kept my heart hammering against my ribs like a caged hummingbird.

"Which one?" Benji asked, giving a deflated laugh. "I'm set for the quizzes next week, but I've got to study up on biochem tonight."

"Once we get back to the hotel we can hit the flash cards."

"Oh, you don't have to worry, Rex."

"Baby, I'm never worried about you." I leaned in for another kiss. I put an arm around his shoulders and let his head fall on mine. "Besides, it helps keep my brain sharp, too. I'm learning all about chemical reactions and animal anatomy and how much coffee a human can conceivably drink before turning into a jittery tap dancer."

Benji laughed, a sound I could never get tired of. "I don't drink *that* much coffee." He sat back up and shrugged. "Sometimes I switch it up with Red Bull."

"Great," I said, arching a brow, smiling. "Even better."

"I'll take the studying help," he said, returning the smile with an even bigger one. The midday sun beamed bright, lighting his face up like a spotlight shining just for him.

God, I was so proud of him. He was a year into vet school and already kicking ass, and even though he was working harder than ever before, he also seemed *happier* than ever before. He not only took control of his depression, but he fucking owned it. He didn't let his life get derailed, even though that would have been the easier option. He inspired me on the daily. If it wasn't for him, I wouldn't have run for local office, and I wouldn't have been voted in. There had been a lot to worry about leading into my decision, but Benji reassured me with every step that it would all turn out okay.

And he was right. Always had been.

My life had gotten better and brighter since the day Benji and I reconnected, and I couldn't be more grateful.

It helped that the sex tape scandal had been dead and buried for over a year now. It was a quick shift, changing from "Senator's son leaked threesome" to "Senator's son, victim of blackmail ring," and it happened when Theo tracked the camera and email back to none other than...

Penelope and fucking Scott. Those two heartless fuckheads who I had trusted enough to explore my sexuality with. They used me, and they used plenty of other people, too.

Theo made the discovery about two days after the tape leaked, and the day after was when police escorted a cuffed Scott and Penelope into the jail. The local news picked up the developments, which quickly went viral through the internet. By then, anyone who hadn't realized the tape was a massive violation of my privacy was quick to see the truth. The narrative shifted, and it was no longer about me being bisexual or having a sex tape, but instead focused on Penelope and Scott, who had made it their living to secretly record people who were in the closet, only to then blackmail them or their families.

It had been a whirlwind few weeks that I'd never forget. But Benji had been at my side through every moment of it.

It wasn't long after that when the situation with the Dove exploded, and it was my turn to be there for

Benji. The Gold family hired Theo, who took the case with as much enthusiasm as he had for mine. We were all confident that he could get to the bottom of things, ending this years-long nightmare for the family.

None of us ever could have imagined how it would actually end.

A raven-haired PA peeked her head in through the door, derailing my train of thought. "Ten minutes until we need you guys onstage." She spoke something into her headset before disappearing again.

"All right," I said, clapping my thighs before standing up. "Let's do this."

I started to get more and more nervous. We were here accepting a Leadership for Change award, my dad only the second person ever to have won it. Since coming out, my dad had more than earned it. Just recently, he fought tooth and nail against a law that would have allowed adoption agencies the right to deny gay parents. It was sobering to see him fight so hard against something that sounded so wrong to me. Such a basic concept—gay parents are just as equal and capable of loving and raising children as their straight counterparts. Yet, for some reason, it had become a polarized issue. Thankfully, my dad now stood on the right side of the fence, not only striking down the law but managing to flip it so that protections for queer parents were now in place across the state.

Now, whenever the time came, Benji and I could go to any adoption agency and not have to worry about being kicked out because we simply loved one another. That was a walk of shame no one should ever have to take, and I'd forever love my dad for making sure no one would ever walk it at all.

But getting up onstage to support my dad wasn't the *only* reason I was getting a bucket of butterflies dumped in my stomach.

I put my hands in my deep pant pockets. My fingers instinctively shut around the soft velvet box that had been pressed against my leg all day, its presence a warm reassurance and a nerve-heightening reminder at the same time.

"You guys are going to be great up there," Benji said, standing, one hand looping through my elbow. He looked into my eyes, smiling wide.

"I love you, Rex."

"And I love you, baby." I kissed him. "Forever."

REX and his dad walked onto the stage to a room full of clapping and cheering. Behind them, the blue-and-white screens shifted and shimmered as if someone waved a magic wand at them, a video of Gavin Madison waving a rainbow flag at a Pride parade taking up the screens as a pop song made us all dance in our seats.

They both seemed excited, beaming from ear to ear as Gavin received his award. Rex resembled a handsome prince up on that stage, taking the spot next to his dad behind the tall glass podium. I looked between them, the stage lights lighting them up like celebrities, seeing a lot of similarities reflected back at me. They both had the same happy-sounding laugh, with the same easygoing grin and bright sky-blue eyes. I remembered a time when I thought the two of them couldn't be any more opposite, and I strongly disliked Gavin for that. I'd seen him as a man who fought against my rights to live a happy life, except that entire time, he was actually fighting against his own inner demons, his struggle manifesting in hurtful ways.

Over the last two years, though, Gavin had really turned himself around. It had been a week or two before he was supposed to win his Senate seat in a landslide. He made a moving speech at the Georgia capitol that caused enough waves to garner international media attention. He came out on a worldwide stage, announcing his divorce of his wife while also making clear his love and support for his son. That part tugged at everyone's heartstrings, even the most ruthless. He had started to cry, and the pain in his voice was real and raw. It resonated. He apologized for hurting him, along with the rest of the queer community. He promised, right there on live TV, that he would work for the rest of his life, wherever it took him, to make life easier for queer kids and adults all around the world.

It was a risky but very much-needed move. To be honest, I didn't think he'd win the votes he needed to hold on to his seat. Although things *seemed* to be moving in the right direction, it was hard to tell how far we'd actually gotten.

Until the votes came in. Then it was clear: we came a hell of a way from where we started.

And since getting re-elected, Gavin immediately put his words into action. He really proved to everyone watching that he meant what he said through his now famous confirmation speech: "Equality for all means *for all*, not for *some*. Not just for those who look or sound or pray like you. *For all*."

It was a resounding rebuke. And he fought every day to make sure queer people were seen as equals all throughout Georgia and beyond.

"Thank you, thank you," Gavin said, the clapping softly dying down. I settled into my seat, trying not to freak out about seeing my boyfriend up on stage while about fifteen famous actors and actresses sat in tables all around me.

"This award really means so much to me. Not

because I never win awards, which does factor into things just a little bit, but because it symbolizes something way bigger than just me. This symbolizes a hopeful shift for all of us. I've been in the closet for forty-two years of my life and almost forgot what being 'hopeful' even feels like.

"I don't want anyone forgetting what 'hope' feels like. I'm committed to making positive change and inspiring a trail of leaders behind me, keeping that change alive even when I won't be able to. So thank you." He put a hand on his heart and bowed his head, the lights reflecting a sheen in his blue eyes.

"And, before they play the music, I wanted to introduce my son, Rex, the main reason why I changed into the better man I am today." Gavin grabbed Rex in a tight hug, and the crowd broke into more applause.

Rex took the mic, and his dad stepped to the side. He seemed nervous, but I think I'd be the only one to tell. It was in the way he twitched his thumb and shuffled his feet. Small signals that I could quickly recognize.

"Hi, y'all." He gave an awkward wave to a room of friendly laughter. "My dad taught me a lot about life, especially in recent years. He taught me to live without thinking of the judgment from others, and he taught me to follow my dreams even when they look impossible to reach. One of those dreams is sitting right there." He pointed directly at me, the spotlight shifting so that I sat under it, surrounded by a sea of darkness. Rex's face smiled at me from the stage.

People were clapping, but I couldn't hear much past the blood pounding in my ears.

"Come up here for a sec, Benj." Rex waved me up, motioning for me to climb onstage. More clapping. Some cheering. Someone nudged my shoulder. Was this really happening? I needed to move.

I stood up, my legs working even though I could feel them shaking. I laughed nervously, climbing up onstage with Rex's help. I didn't even look out at the crowd, terrified I would lock eyes with one of my favorite actors and instantly melt into a puddle spelling out "fan girl."

Rex turned to me, looking only at me. The room seemed to collapse inward, the crowd and their hushed murmurs disappearing. I locked eyes with those ocean-blue orbs I'd fallen so deeply in love with.

"Benji," he said, loud enough for the mic to pick up. "You've also taught me so much. How to take control of life and not let it take control of you. You've taught me how to tell the difference between a coral snake and a king snake—red touches yellow you're a dead fellow, red touches black, you're okay, Jack."

"Correct," I said, the room breaking in laughter.

"But beyond all that, you taught me how to love again. How to love you, how to love myself, how to love life."

Wait, what was he doing? Why was he dropping down? Why was he putting a knee on the ground? Why was he reaching into—

"Benjamin Francis Gold, will you continue loving life with me?"

He opened up a navy blue box, and inside it sat a gleaming silver band, taking my breath away.

"Will you marry me?"

Silence swept through the room. Ice clinking against glass could be heard.

Shock. I was shocked and overwhelmed and absolutely over the fucking moon.

"Yes," I said, low at first, realizing only the front of the room probably heard. So I said it louder, my happiness overflowing. "Yes, Rex, yes, absolutely yes!"

The room erupted into the loudest round of applause and cheers yet. People were up on their feet as Rex slid the ring on my finger, a perfect fit. He stood up, his expression a mixture of relief and overwhelming excitement. He grabbed me in a tight hug and kissed me, the cheers continuing.

"Forever," he said against my lips.

"Forever," I replied, feeling the ring on my finger, excited to see what forever would bring us.

THE END.

THANK you for reading *VELVET MIDNIGHT.* If you enjoyed the conclusion to Benji and Rex's story then consider leaving a review! And keep a lookout for the next book following Maverick and Theo as they work to finally figure out who the Dove is (and fall deeply and irrevocably in love along the way).

Receive access to a bundle of my **free stories** by signing up for my newsletter!

Tap here to sign up for my newsletter.

Be sure to connect with me on Instagram and Twitter **@maxwalkerwrites.** And join my Facebook Group: Mad for Max Walker

Max Walker
MaxWalkerAuthor@outlook.com

ALSO BY MAX WALKER

The Gold Brothers

Hummingbird Heartbreak

Velvet Midnight

The Stonewall Investigation Series

A Hard Call

A Lethal Love

A Tangled Truth

A Lover's Game

OR

Books 1-4 Box Set

The Stonewall Investigation- Miami Series

Bad Idea

Lie With Me

His First Surrender

The Sierra View Series

Code Silver

Code Red

Code Blue

Code White

The Guardian Series

Books 1-4 Box Set

Audiobooks:

A Hard Call - narrated by Greg Boudreaux

A Lethal Love - narrated by Greg Boudreaux

A Tangled Truth - narrated by Greg Boudreaux

A Lover's Game - narrated by Greg Boudreaux

Deck the Halls - narrated by Greg Boudreaux

Code Silver - narrated by Jason Frazier

Christmas Stories:

Daddy Kissing Santa Claus

Daddy, It's Cold Outside

Deck the Halls

Printed in Great Britain
by Amazon

56132753R00180